TOXIC DESIRE

TOXIC DESIRE

ROBIN LOVETT

This book is a work of fiction. Names, characters, places, and incidents are the product of the author's imagination or are used fictitiously. Any resemblance to actual events, locales, or persons, living or dead, is coincidental.

Copyright © 2018 by Robin Lovett. All rights reserved, including the right to reproduce, distribute, or transmit in any form or by any means. For information regarding subsidiary rights, please contact the Publisher.

Entangled Publishing, LLC
2614 South Timberline Road
Suite 105, PMB 159
Fort Collins, CO 80525
Visit our website at www.entangledpublishing.com.

Scorched is an imprint of Entangled Publishing, LLC.

Edited by Tracy Montoya
Cover design by Cover Couture
Cover art from Shutterstock and Deposit Photos

Manufactured in the United States of America

First Edition March 2018

entangled
scorched

Chapter One

Nem

I'm slammed against the wall, and I squeeze my leg up between our bodies before he crushes me. And when I say crush me, I don't mean in a sexy way. I mean he will literally pound my face in or drive a knife between my ribs.

Good thing I'm wearing shellskin armor.

He, however, is not.

I thrust my booted foot into his gut, and with a heavy grunt, he stumbles backward, hitting the opposite metal wall with a bang.

Damn, that had to hurt.

Score one for me.

I dive for the blaster he kicked from my hand—the warning systems of my ship's computer blaring: *"Evacuate. Evacuate. This is not a drill. Find the nearest escape pod. This is not a drill."* She's going down, fast being pulled into the gravity of the nearest planet and burning from the inside out. And it's all because of him—him and his looting barbarians—sneaking on board, setting fire to the reactor.

My hands close around the blaster, and I level it at him, aiming for the center of his chest. At least six of my crew are dead. I will have no remorse in adding him to the pile.

"Your weapon will not work on me," he drones. His bass voice resonates in the hall over the alarm. How that's possible, I don't know.

"It works on everything. Even you." My voice sounds hollow, toneless from the voice scrambler that disguises my sex. I sound as inhuman as he is. Between that, my shapeless armor and my helmet screen, no one can tell I'm female. Not even my crew—who are hopefully already propelling from this doomed vessel for the nearest habitable ecosystem.

He doesn't freeze like he should with a weapon aimed at him, and he doesn't pull out a blaster of his own. The leather holsters crisscrossing his massive pectorals contain knives of varying lengths, sheathed and available for him to grab.

He stretches his shoulders and flexes his chest. "There is a reason why your entire species is afraid of my kind."

"Fairy stories." I don't care how bright gold and incandescent his skin. It's penetrable. No matter what the tales tell about his kind being unkillable. I've got a laser.

He steps toward me. "Go ahead. Try it." His accent is strange, his tongue rolling over the consonants in a thick burr.

I should shoot. Now. But my trigger finger hesitates.

I don't want him dead yet. I need to find out, how did he do it?

How did he and his band of brutes get onto my ship without my knowing? How did he accomplish what no other army or species in the Ten Systems has managed to do—catch me?

I have to know. "How did you get on board this ship?"

He pauses. "You invaded our sanctum airspace. You must have expected retaliation." His dark eyes narrow into slits so menacing they send shivers down my spine. I don't know what species he is, but he fits the stories I heard in childhood: the Ssedez descended from serpents, glowing like sphinxes, with fangs dripping in venom capable of making someone a slave to their desire in one bite. Well, thank gods, his teeth seem normal enough, so that last part is likely myth.

But he cannot be a Ssedez. I don't care how godlike his proportioned body is—as though every muscle is chiseled and lined out of fine marble. It has to be coincidence how rigid and angular his jaw is. The Ssedez were destroyed a century ago by the Ten Systems.

"Who are you?" I ask, unable to contain my curiosity. "What do you want with us?" My ship, the *Origin*, groans another warning. I can't believe it's time to abandon her, but we have to—or die.

He snarls, and his voice drops another octave as he hisses and strains to pronounce the words. "We want the same thing for you that you want for us: annihilation."

Something odd happens to me that has never happened and isn't supposed to happen.

Not only am I not afraid of him, but I become aware, physically, that he is male, I am female, and that I haven't had sex since…

I can't remember.

It shouldn't matter. I'm a general, a ship captain, a career soldier, with ambitions that leave no time for personal anything. Physical desire serves no purpose in my life.

But the ruthlessness in him, the ferocious gleam in his eyes—it excites me.

The symmetry of his bone structure alone is blinding. The ferocious angles of his cheeks and jaw are paired with an otherworldly elegance in the gold sheen of his complexion. I'm glad my helmet hides that my eyes are wide in fascination.

His hair gleams, too, like it's laced with gold flecks. The

strands hang to his shoulders, unbound, a contradiction. He's an untamed beast formed with siren-like beauty.

He moves, his lethal muscles stirring inside that gloriously brilliant body.

"Don't come any closer," I warn, grateful for the scrambler that hides the shaking in my voice.

His body is physically distracting. Hard, like metallic hard, and big. He is all brawn and possession—the epitome of conqueror in strength as well as deed. And it's not just his chest and arms. Even his thighs, outlined in black leather, are thickly muscled and bulging. It has me hungering for a glimpse of what is no doubt equally impressive between them. And wondering if what's between his thighs is as godlike as the rest of him.

Apparently, despite decades of denying it, there's enough hetero-female left in me to know if I wasn't supposed to kill him, I would want him to fuck me. Now.

He stalks toward me.

"Stop!" I shout, tightening my grip on the blaster. He will not get closer. The ship jerks, and we're both thrown off balance. I brace myself against a doorway.

"Your ship will not last long, General Nem." He knows my name and rank. Which he could only get from hacking my ship's computer. "Your crew are dead. Like you should be."

I will not react and give him more of an advantage.

My crew aren't all dead. Some already escaped in emergency vessels. But I'm not telling him that.

I realign my blaster for where his heart should be, if he has one. "*You'll* be dead if you don't tell me how you got aboard my ship!" Unlike him and his alluringly resonant voice, I have to shout to be heard over the rising alarms.

"No leader wants to find out he has a traitor on board."

The blood in my veins runs with ice. A *traitor?* "No one in my crew would betray me!"

"Take one more step behind you, General, and I'll tell you who did."

I know what door is behind me. "Why would I get in an escape pod with you?" I refuse to let him out of this alive. I have to get to the docking bay and off this ship to join my crew.

I have to grab one thing, though, first.

I rub my finger on the blaster's trigger. Why haven't I killed this bastard?

He straightens from the wall. "I will tell you everything about the Ssedez you humans have wanted to know but have never been able to understand."

He *is* one of them!

My heart jumps, and I have to reassert my blaster aim. I can't let him know I've been hunting for other species like his. It's the whole point of the *Origin's* mission. "You'll kill me."

A growl rumbles through his chest, but he nods. "And then I will kill you."

I squeeze the trigger, and the neon green bolt of light hits him in the torso, too fast for him to dodge. He should fall. I expect him to land on the deck.

But to my horror, his skin illuminates with the light. He turns bright gold, every part of him glowing. With a roar, he comes at me, body slams me, throwing us into the escape pod.

I twist before I hit the floor, going for a headlock. But he wrenches away from me, moving with a litheness that shouldn't be possible for a being of his size.

He punches the flashing red button by the door.

And before I have time to scream, it closes with a *whoosh*, and we're detached, hurtling through space.

Chapter Two

Oten

We are thrust from Nem's ship in a pod, tumbling free into space. I stretch for handholds to anchor myself, so I do not bang into the walls.

I may not need armor, but my bones can still break.

Nem shouts but gives up hope of killing me. His blaster will not work on me any more than that worthless full-body armor of his. I cannot even see his face. It angers me when I cannot see my enemies' eyes as I kill them.

I expect the pod to fire off to where my ship—my Ssedez warriors—will easily capture us. There, I will be reunited, and we can do to this human what is best. Torture him for everything he knows about the humans—whether others are coming, and if his kind knows we still exist or if he is a lone ship gone astray. Then we will give him as brutal a death as his Ten Systems' army gave Ssedez civilians when they started a war and attacked our cruisers over a century ago.

Except the pod does not float into space.

It speeds, gathering momentum, forcing us against the curved back wall of the vessel, gravity trapping us. Which only means one thing—we are being pulled toward a planet.

And the only planet near enough is Fyrian.

The fire world. To enter its atmosphere is to incinerate. It means death.

I thank the gods I have no spouse or children to leave behind.

I have no regrets. The human, though I would rather kill him with my bare hands, will die with me.

Heat, hot, sweat, burning. The interior of the pod shakes and hums. Not even the defensive armor of my skin—impervious to any weaponry—can shield me from fire.

So this is what it feels like to be burned alive.

The human does not scream or cry out in pain, and, though I must grind my teeth, I do not, either. I focus on my dying prayer—that none of my warriors escaping the ship will suffer the same fate as me.

Death comes with a jolt to my body like thunder ripping through my chest, and the last thing I feel is a hammer pounding of my head.

I awake...

Gasping, my lungs screaming, sucking on air that is not air at all. It is nothing—nothing that my lungs process anyhow. The pod is pitch dark; no light shines, except for a flashing button that blinks EJECT. In a firing of instinct, I crawl with my burning body to the control console and hit the button.

The hatch opens. Blinding sunlight and a rush of air explode against my face, but it is so hot, it knocks me unconscious again.

What wakes me is water dripping into my eyes—which

turns out to be condensation dripping from the pod.

I wipe it away, then force myself to my feet. Though I am sweltering as in a sauna, I look down at my limbs, and I have not burned. My armor remains untarnished. I retract it, pulling the protective covering back into my skin.

It seethes like a fire in my belly from the nexus of my spine. My lungs ache from the burn, and my vision pulses with a red haze.

I do not understand what I am feeling.

I stumble out of the pod into a jungle. Green and more green as far as I can see. Enormous vegetation with leaves bigger than my head. Trees thick as three of me, trunks overgrown with vines, and moss so richly dark a green, it's almost blue. And humid.

The air is so thick with fog, it could be steam.

My muscles heat like coals, and the holsters confining my chest are unbearable. I unbuckle them, fingers shaking with impatience, and feel as though my skin will burst into blisters.

Something stirs beside me. My reaction is slow, my gaze heavy, and limbs lethargic with the fire racing through my blood.

The creature dressed in black, the general, the human, rouses, and a fury starts in my core, the flames singeing through my veins blazing.

His breathing is harsh and labored, so loud, I can hear it from inside his helm. He reaches for it, fingers fumbling in gloves, frantic. His groan of frustration is a sound so desperate and guttural, it shoots through me like the laser he shot at me on the ship.

The blaze coursing in me intensifies and pulses through every part of me, including my loins, which swell and strain. And I know not why.

But then he removes his helm. Or...

She.

That is why.

Her hair is cut to her chin, but her bone structure, her face, is an array of delicate cheekbones and full lips. Panting heavily, sweat dripping from her face, she pulls at her armor, yanking it off until she's left wearing a white clinging suit—which is barely a covering at all. It molds over her chest, revealing high and tight breasts with round, rubied nipples outlined against the fabric.

She tears off her gloves and stands to full height, rubbing at her body, scratching over her limbs. She feels it, too, this burn, this heat. It is as though she is trying to wipe it off her. Her movements are frenetic—crossing over her hips and thighs. A grimace strains her features, and she grips her breasts hard and squeezes, as though trying to relieve a pain.

It is the same for me, though mine is a pain to be doing to her exactly as she is doing to herself. To stroke her and feel her against me. To possess her body with my hands.

Why I want to do this to a human is odd, and I do not understand my own desire.

She releases one breast and drags her hand down her belly to press between her legs. The sound she makes is the most sexual thing I have ever heard.

Her gaze lands on me and, there is no surprise or anger at seeing her enemy. There is only hunger.

"You are female," I rumble.

"And your…your…mouth." Her words are broken by gasps, and she writhes against her hand and stares at my mouth. With a delicate tongue, she licks her lips.

I mirror the gesture—try to lick mine—but instead feel my fangs descending.

Venom drips from the tips lengthening past my lip. The intoxicant tastes sweet on my tongue, but in a sickly way. The venom isn't meant for me to taste; it's an aphrodisiac meant for her.

She tilts her head, exposing the column of her throat. A carnal need to bite her seizes me. There are reasons why I should not, many reasons why this is wrong. Something is not right. None of this should be.

Something about this planet, the air, the heat, the steam, is fucking with us. I force my gaze away from her and try to focus on what is around me.

"What is this place?" I pant in her language, trying to think of anything but how my body feels.

"I...don't...know." Her voice is tight with pain.

I glance back at her, and it is obvious she is trying not to look at me. But it does not matter that she is my worst enemy whom I have trained my whole life to kill.

And when she looks back at me, it does not seem to matter to her either that I just destroyed her ship and killed off a lot of her crew. Her gaze drags over my body with the kind of need that echoes mine.

"What is...happening?" she gasps, her breathing rapid. "This...is...awful."

"I do not know."

The fire scorching through me burns away my ability to care why I should not want her. My mind is useless. The only way I can think to quench the flames within me is to sink my fangs into her.

She sucks air through her teeth. "Bite me."

I am incapable of resisting her command.

I grab her and haul her to me.

She clings to me and leans her head back, exposing her throat once more.

I bite, my fangs cutting into her flesh in one fast strike. She cries out and crushes my head closer to her, sinking my fangs deeper.

The ecstasy is excruciating. The venom streams from my mouth into her vein; the convulsions start—whether in me or in her I do not know.

We are on the ground; I am on top of her, our bodies writhing, animal and greedy. My cock aches and pounds too hard for me to even think of undressing her, of opening her legs, and fucking into her cunt with all the ruthlessness with which she is grinding against me.

A scream of pleasure rings from her throat, and she thrusts against me, her thighs vising my hips. The clothes separating us do not matter. I have to come.

I orgasm so hard I have to detach from her throat to let out my own climatic shouts. It slices through my gut and short-circuits my brain.

Rewired, unmade, I collapse over her and fall into blissful unconsciousness.

Chapter Three

Nem

He bit me. I asked him to. He gave me an orgasm. I made him come, too.

At least the burning stopped.

Or dulled.

The heat lessens, and I am grateful. I don't care what I had to do to get it to stop. I don't care that the man—or male Ssedez—who destroyed my ship and half my crew had to lie on top of me. I don't care that I begged him to bite me and fell victim to…to…to whatever the hell his fangs did to me.

And his body—all the rippling gold muscle in my hands, over me, trapping me—

Damn, it was good. Whatever it was. I don't care that I should've killed him already—at the moment, anyway. That will change.

This isn't me. I don't do this. I'm a career military woman. I don't fuck the enemy.

I don't fuck anyone.

I'm dedicated to my crew. My mission is everything to me. My entire life, everything my family sacrificed, the future of the universe, could depend on what I was forced to leave behind on that ship.

I don't know what the hell this planet is doing to me. I can't fathom how it's making me lose my focus, but this bullshit stops now.

At least I no longer feel like I'm on fire from the inside out. That was the most excruciating pain… Followed by the most blissed-out orgasm ever. But whatever. I'll block that out.

When my will to move returns, I push him off me and get away from him. I lean on my knees and breathe, nauseous. And I am horrified to feel a dull heat simmering in my core—that can't be the burn still there.

But I slip my hand between my legs and rub myself—it sends a jolt up my spine.

"What the hell?" I shout at the ground. I'm still swollen. This can't be happening. I rarely think about, much less need, sex—an intentional by-product of my bioengineering. But it doesn't seem to work here.

Images of him and his fangs—what it would've been like if he'd taken off his leather pants and torn off my clothes. What his cock would've felt like, the one I felt between our layers of fabric, as big and hard as he is, thrusting into me. That body of loaded gold muscle fucking me.

His skin was smooth under my hands. And cool. A refreshing cool next to my steaming skin.

His hair—I touched it. The shining strands look coarse. The gold metallic appearance is deceptive. They were luxurious and soft.

I want to touch it again. I want to twist my hands in his hair while he fucks me mercilessly.

I come against my own hand. It's a murmur of a climax

compared to the one he gave me, but it clears my mind briefly enough to remember…

He is my enemy.

And I am unarmed.

I glance back at him, and he is watching me, his hand massaging himself through the leather he wears. He totally saw me make myself come again.

I force myself to focus. No matter how badly I'm craving to see what his cock looks like, there are more important things I need.

All my weapons were attached to my armor, which is now lying helter skelter—and he is between me and it.

I spot his chest holsters lying on the ground and grab them. Their weight is significant; the pouches must hold more than knives, likely explosives by the heft. I stand, unsheathe the fiercest looking blade, and face him.

He's still sitting. He's stopped touching his cock, but his gaze is far from someone at a disadvantage. Which I suppose is true. He could swipe a leg at my ankles and bring me down.

Not that I'd let that happen.

"Are you going to kill me now?" He nods at his knife in my hand.

I shake off the chill his voice sends through me. "I should."

"Would've been smarter to do while I was in thrall."

"I enthrall you?" I'm too shocked to play coy with it.

He makes a grunting sound and stands. I don't miss how his gaze sweeps over me as he does. It lingers over my thighs and hips.

He stares at my neck. "That was not an attempt to kill you, I will say."

I touch the two puncture wounds on the side of my throat. "I surmised as much."

"If you let me lick it, it will heal faster." His voice lowers, even softens.

The thought of him touching me, let alone with his mouth, has heat flooding my veins—again. "I'll heal on my own, thanks. My bioengineering is more advanced than that."

His breath shudders, and he forces his gaze from me. "Your choice."

I don't know what to do. He's made no violent advances toward me. But I can hardly let my guard down.

"What is this place?" he asks, looking at the environment. "This is nothing like we supposed Fyrian would be."

"Fyrian?"

"This planet. The fire world."

"The fire world?"

"Its atmosphere is a haze of red. From space, we believed it engulfed in flames."

I recall the star charts aboard my ship. "You mean Planet 6542. It's caused by a gas releasing from the planet's core."

"Is it toxic?" He puts his hand to his chest. "This burning feeling. It is being caused by something." He feels it, too. His gaze barely manages to stay on my face, drifting to my nipples and back to my lips.

And this is why, even after I went rogue with my crew and could've abolished the gender-free regulation, I did not. If the others know I'm female, it changes everything, from how they speak to me to how they look at me. Best to just require everyone to wear their helms, armor, and voice scramblers. Then everyone is the same, and there is no sexist treatment.

But now, thanks to this damn "fire planet" heat thing and my armor's inability to cope with the temperature, I've let my enemy know my secret.

No orgasm, no matter how good, is worth that.

"Eyes on my face when you're talking to me." I point his knife at his chest.

Something happens to his skin. It goes from smooth as

mine to a thick texture, a diamond pattern slipping over the surface like a protective covering. Almost like scales. Almost like a serpent.

"What the..." My knife hand falters, and he seizes my lapse in attention.

He grabs my wrist, keeping me from bringing the knife closer. "Unlike you, I do not require external armor."

I could test it. My knife work is good. I could release his hold and slice his forearm open. I could find out if his natural armor is as impenetrable as my shellskin armor was.

But his touch, the smoothness of his palm—he slides it down my forearm beneath the sleeve covering it. He strokes me with the pads of his fingers, and I become aware how soft my skin is. And how much he likes it.

"Why did you hide your sex?" he asks. "Female warriors among Ssedez are rare and treasured."

That breaks my hypnosis. "To be treasured is to be inferior." I jerk my hand back. "I am a soldier." I turn toward the escape pod.

But by some trick of his fingers, he disarms me.

I stare back at his hand, the knife I was holding now grasped there. I'm forced to concede his knife skills are superior to mine. Which I shouldn't take as a blow to my pride—knives are obviously his primary weapon—but I don't like being inferior in anything.

"Those belong to me." He nods at his holsters still in my other hand. His tone is deceptively casual; his stance, however, is ready to do battle.

There's a cache of weapons, my kind of weapons, in the bunker inside the pod. I calculate how fast I can get to them. It's a game of chance. I don't want to appear hostile. We have a good truce going on here, and logic says we'll survive this foreign planet better as a pair than alone.

"If you really want to try and kill me, go get your

weapons." He nods toward the pod's interior.

"If I were a man, you wouldn't give me that chance. This is why I hide my sex."

"You're upset that I give you mercy?"

"I don't want your mercy."

He steps closer, invading my space, towering over me, though his knife is lowered. He's not pointing it at me, but he could in an instant. "What do you want?"

"I want you dead." Or that's what I wanted before. It's what I should still want.

His eyes flash as though he finds this exciting. "Then why am I still alive?" It's a taunt. He doesn't think I would kill him. "You want more, don't you?"

I growl, pissed at myself for not killing him. Pissed at him for knowing why.

He leans his mouth down to my ear. "You may not like me knowing you're female, but since I do, you're dying to be fucked."

Anger seethes in me, and I swing his ten-pound holsters at his head. He ducks in time, but it throws him off balance. It leaves me an opening, and I charge him.

Even his big frame is no match for the full impact of my body slam. I knock him to the ground and snatch another knife from his holsters. I get the blade to his neck.

But not before he gets his knife to mine.

Stalemate.

He chuckles low in his chest.

"What's funny?" I say. "I'm as likely to kill you as you are me."

"Go ahead. Try to cut me. See what happens."

Curious, I press the blade against his skin, but it scrapes over the protective covering and—nothing happens. No give, no indentation.

I'm baffled, and in my surprise, he gets the better of me

and flips me onto my back.

He knocks the wind from my lungs and traps my legs with his. "And since you took your armor off, you are at my mercy now."

I struggle but only briefly. He's trapped me. He learned my move of pressing him away with my leg. My other mainstay, breaking his nose with my forehead, isn't an option with a blade at my throat. "Bastard."

"I do not plan to kill you. Not yet. I need information from you. And I need you to operate the support systems on that pod, because I do not know how."

I grasp his hand, testing his strength against mine. He doesn't budge. "You need me for more than that. Admit it."

The burn is heating inside me again. Having him on top of me makes it worse. The weight of him has me hungering for another of his mind-bending orgasms—except this time with him fucking me.

I shift my hips and feel his cock hard against my belly. Long and thick. It could be its flaccid state. I don't know, but going by the heat in his eyes, it's not.

A growl rumbles low in his chest, and he fingers the puncture wounds on my neck. They'll heal before the day is over. All trace of them will be gone by morning. But he stares at the marks, and his mouth parts to reveal his fangs lowering again. I watch them protrude past his lip, his tongue licking the tips.

His tongue—it's forked.

If I wasn't enflamed between my legs, I am now. With my thighs pressed together between his legs, a wetness seeps onto them. I can't help it—not with the thought of his dual tongue tips licking through the thick folds between my thighs.

I whimper, and I can't believe the sound is coming from me.

I close my eyes and turn my head away, forcing myself to

breathe.

He gets off of me.

I sit up, resting my head between my knees. Whoever this person is, this me who craves sex like she needs air, I don't know her. She is foreign, and I don't know how to deal with her.

My anger at myself twists my stomach almost as hard as my hatred for him does. It's his damn fault we're in this mess—his brutality that destroyed my entire life's mission.

And this gods-forsaken planet that has me hungrier for sex with him than for a desire to get revenge and kill him.

It has to be something about this place causing me to feel this way.

I need answers. I stalk to the pod and pull its portable computer from the control console. Whatever is in the atmosphere burning through my lungs and veins has to be causing this.

There's no other reason why I would want to fuck this male who has cost me everything.

Chapter Four

Oten

Tasting my venom again sets off warnings in my head. I did not think about it the first time, because my blood was on fire. But the venom is not something I have tasted since I was a pubescent youth, not for a hundred and twenty-five years. It is not something that happens with just any sexual encounter.

It is only supposed to happen at the initiation of the Attachment.

Which cannot be. She is not even Ssedez, of my own species. She is human, and therefore denies the ethic of life and freedom to any people not her own. I cannot be forming a mating bond to her.

But my body, now that I have bitten her, literally has begun to believe she is my mate for life.

Which is impossible. And yet the venom does not lie.

Nor does my deluded urge to protect her. Or the fact that holding her at knifepoint made me sick to my stomach.

Unthinkable.

It must be this place.

The feelings cannot be true.

The Attachment will never be completed. There are other steps involved. My heart and soul have to form an intimate bond as well as my body. My self-preservation instinct has to morph into a willing-to-sacrifice-my-life-for-her commitment.

None of those things have happened. And never will. So once I get away from her, the physical bond will disintegrate.

It has to. That is the only option.

I just have to survive this urge to bite her again. And the need to fuck her senseless.

A sonic boom draws my eyes to the sky.

And there I see a horrifying, surreal sight—General Nem's starship.

It is so large, it almost seems to float, but it must be falling near the speed of sound. I hear a gasp behind me, and she is there, watching.

Her mouth falls open on a silent, "No," and her expression is a vulnerable sea of shock. I should be rejoicing. This is what we intended when we boarded her ship. To destroy it.

But instead, I feel sorrow.

Which I should not feel. She is the enemy.

I have no shame over what I have done. The Ten Systems' army she takes orders from, they murdered a million Ssedez, attacking us mercilessly on our home world and in space, attempting genocide.

After fifty years of war and death, we decided to fake our extinction and vacate our home world. We settled on a new one in a different system—one unknown to our enemies.

Until now, when Nem flies her ship into our airspace.

But that ship is no more. Thanks to me and to my warriors.

A quake of land-moving force shakes the ground beneath our feet. In the sky, the bow of her ship has hit the planet surface, and the stern falls backward until the ship disappears beyond the tree-filled horizon, followed by another quake.

Then silence.

Even the jungle's creatures are quiet.

I feel a sense of completion. Mission accomplished, without loss of Ssedez life or exposure of the location of our new world.

But it is not a sweet victory. Not like it should be. Because of her.

She hides it well in the set of her mouth, but the shimmer in her eyes gives it away. Losing her ship is a catastrophic loss. It would be for me as well.

But when her gaze shifts to me, it floods with hatred. "You." Her voice is more gravelly than any voice scrambler could make it. "How many of my crew are dead because of you?"

I am stunned; she is more feeling than I thought. She cares more about the people who are likely dead than she does for her ship. "Many."

"Why?" she screams. "We did nothing to you!"

My lip curls in a snarl. "You humans attempted to destroy my entire species."

"We were traveling peacefully through universal airspace!"

"In a warship!"

"We've made no aggressive maneuvers since entering the system. Nothing we did gave you cause for attacking us!"

"Your existence gives me cause to destroy you."

And yet I haven't. I could kill her now. Torture her for what she knows. Get it over with. But the thought of doing that, of hurting her, reviles me. A war wages within me. My heart, which still aches for the loved ones I lost in the war, wants to see her blood on the ground.

My body, though, will not allow me to lift a knife to her.

It would be so easy. Without her armor, she is so vulnerably mortal. One slice of my knife and she would be dead. Unless she fought me off first. She might.

I cannot do it. I cannot hurt her.

"Why am I still alive then?" she says, her voice low.

"Because I am not ready to kill you yet."

"Then I guess I'll find a way to kill you first." She retrieves the holster from her armor and fastens it around her hips. It is stocked with weapons, not all of which I recognize, and watching her buckle it is akin to a physical taunt.

Her skin is so pale; she's obviously spent zero time in the sun and most of her life in space.

The white suit she wears, that her armor hid before, accentuates the curve of her hips and the muscle tone of her body.

The heat, the flames, reignite within me. Gone are the horrors and spoils of war, the threats of who is killing whom. She is female, and I am the male who wants to claim her.

I want to strip her and make her come. To feel her body writhe in ecstasy on my hand, on my mouth, on my cock.

I step forward to reach for her, but she grabs the blaster at her waist and warns, "Don't even think about it."

"That won't—"

"I know it won't kill you, but it will slow you down." She tilts her head curiously. "And I wonder how many shots you can actually withstand. It's self-charging. I'll never run out."

She disappears back inside the pod.

I force myself to stay where I am. If I move, I will go after her.

She comes back out with a large pack and a little touch-pad computer in her hand. "I was right." She rattles off a foreign name of a chemical compound I do not recognize. "The air is filled with it, and its effects on life-forms are unknown."

"How can your computer know it exists but not know its effects?"

She ignores me, goes to a plant, and rips off a piece of leaf. "Shit." Her hand comes away bloody, like the plant cut her, but she inserts a piece of it into her computer. It makes a processing noise then beeps. "It's in the vegetation, too." She sucks the cut on her finger.

"Why did it cut you?"

"I don't know." She stands and points in the direction where her ship landed. "What I do know is where I'm going."

"I will come, too." My warriors will assume I died in the planet's atmosphere. There is no rescue party coming for me. The only hope I have of getting off this rock will be from her human friends. Or any locals who might inhabit this place.

That is the reason why I have resisted killing her, I tell myself.

She does not look at me but shoves the pack at me. "Carry this. It's survival supplies." Then she ventures straight into the jungle.

I shoulder her pack and follow, glad at least she now seems unaffected by the burn that is once more blazing through my veins like fire. Without her begging me for it, it should be easier to ignore it and keep my hands off her.

We walk through the jungle, and I adjust to a perpetual state of arousal. My eyes fill with the sight of her ass in front of me. The well-muscled cheeks move beneath the fabric that molds to her like a second skin.

My cock aches to the point of pain, and my fangs, no matter what mind games I play with myself, will not retract. I cannot bite her again. I will not. It is a betrayal of the rituals of my kind to share venom without Attachment.

It is sacred. To give it to someone who is not one's mate is sacrilege.

To give it to a human…

I am revolted by my inability to control myself in this place. I gave my venom to her. I have never given it to anyone. Not in all my life have I met a Ssedez who called my fangs and venom from me, and not for lack of trying.

For it to happen now with this human is a cruel curse.

We push through the overgrown jungle. Vines and vegetation crawl up the massive trees so densely I cannot see the trunks. The mist is ever present, like walking through fog. The smell of growing things is so potent in the air it floods my nostrils.

The sounds of the animals are loud in our ears. Strange and ethereal chirps and squawks, most hidden and unseen, though very few I recognize from any other planet.

The leaves in various shades of green, purple, and blue—which merely scratch my skin and leather pants—slice holes through her white suit. Boots protect our feet and ankles. But after her suit is torn, the leaves cut her skin until trails of blood drip down her legs.

It stirs the Attachment in me.

I cannot allow anything to hurt her.

Chapter Five

Nem

I'm no stranger to pain. I've been wounded in battle countless times. I've been beaten. I've been scarred. I've been imprisoned. But I have never felt a burning like this.

Each time a leaf cuts me, I grit my teeth. There is nothing I can do. We have to get to my ship. There are valuable things on board, priceless things. If there's any chance they're retrievable, I have to get them. Not to mention the small hope someone on my crew survived the crash. Though it's unlikely. What's more likely is another escape pod landed nearby. No alerts of other pods have shown on my computer, but it doesn't mean they're not there.

Anyone else will head to the crash site.

But the cuts—it's not the tear of my skin so much as the fire that starts at each wound, a burn of intense pleasure. I have to glance down to be sure actual flames aren't creeping up my legs.

"Here. Take this." The Ssedez puts his longest knife in

my hand, and I don't have to ask what it's for. It's not for killing him.

It's long enough to carve a path for myself. A machete. I slice at the leaves ahead of me, bushwhacking through the jungle. It's too late though.

My blood is already contaminated with the plants' poison.

I start to hallucinate. I start seeing *him* in front of me—naked—and I want to cut my teeth on him. I want to get on my knees and suck his cock, then bend over on all fours while he fucks me from behind.

But that's not even the best of the illusions.

In the next one, he bites me and does it all over again—except this time it's twice as good.

I stumble, my body aflame, my nipples hard and scratching against the fabric of my body suit, my clit swollen and aching. Molten from fire scourging my veins, I'm dripping onto my thighs—soaking my clothes.

I stop, drop his knife, and start to touch myself. I need to make it stop. I have to make this end. I will incinerate if I don't quench it somehow.

I fall to my knees. I'm urged backward against a strong chest, and masculine hands come around to replace mine. The broad fingers massage and caress my nipples.

"Harder." I arch into his touch. He obeys, squeezing and twisting the points of my breasts.

It doesn't ease me though. My clit throbs, and I tear one of his hands from my breasts and put it there. "Help me."

His long fingers press me, and I cry out. I have no patience for waiting—I'm in too much pain. I grasp his wrist and use his hand, circling his fingers the way I want them to.

But it's not enough; it still hurts. It blurs my thoughts, and I moan nonsensical things, unable to think except for what I need.

He gropes to find the hidden zipper in my suit, opens it,

and sneaks his hand inside. His hot hand slips between my soaked thighs, and a loud groan vibrates from his chest into my back.

I don't care about his reaction though; all I care is that he makes me come.

I collapse back against him and spread my knees, opening, letting him deeper. He strokes through my folds, and his fingers slip inside me like butter. My inner walls cling to him, squeezing him, desperate to wring the orgasm from his hand.

He slides his fingers in and out of me, their size and width the perfect size of a cock, and I'm so wet, I hear the sounds of him moving them in me. From this pose, I can watch, so I stare at his ethereally gold, shining hand, his palm so broad, his wrist so thick, the muscles of his knuckles flexing and tightening as he works me.

"Faster, faster," I breathe between shuddering breaths, and he obeys. I grip his forearms, digging my fingers as hard as I can into his corded muscle. I start to come, my hips pumping shamelessly onto his hand.

The climax sets off in me like a bomb, wringing harsh shouts from my lungs and seizing my body. I lose it all—the battles, the will for control, the fight to stay alive. I don't care.

I am sex. And pleasure.

The fire that was raging through my veins lessens, and I surrender against his chest. I lie back wasted, lungs heaving, and notice his breathing. It gusts against my ear, and he is as rigid as a statue behind me, his cock a steely, unmistakable force against my back.

He moves like he wants to get away from me, so I crawl forward. I'm too weak to stand, but I rest on my knees. I manage to close the zipper at my waist, not that the clothes are doing me any good, they're so soaked from me and sliced with cuts from the leaves.

I turn to see him standing and staring at me—his cock at eye level.

He looks at me with sensually dark eyes like he wants to fuck me, but at the same time, he's cautious. My caution is gone. My rational restraint is disintegrated. I'm forced to admit that in all my years of curiosity about the Ssedez, I never dared hope I'd actually meet one. Much less have the opportunity to have sex with one. They're supposed to be extinct.

This whole mission of mine—the one he ruined—was all about leaving the Ten Systems and breaking away from their "Assimilate or Be Conquered" rule of law. My crew, our goal is one of discovering worlds and species unknown. Of finding things in common with intelligent life-forms—not dominating others in war.

It is my life's work. And this enemy of mine who brings me so much pleasure is a specimen of my heart's desire.

"What's your name?" Nothing like getting orgasms from a male without knowing his name.

"Oten." The guttural sound to his voice, it fills me with new arousal. The first word I've heard him say in his own language. I don't know how he knows my human language so well, but he's obviously studied it intensively. His name, Oten, is harsh and gritty sounding, the stop on the "T" like a preparation for something ominous. And it is. I recognize it.

"Oten?" I gasp. "As in..." My mind must be playing tricks on me.

"Have you heard the stories of the Ssedez?"

"Are you *the* Oten?" I catch my breath, remembering all I can of the story. "As in the warrior who created the stars of the universe with refracted light across his skin?"

"That tale formed a thousand years ago and refers to my father." He strokes my face, as though enamored with the feel of my skin. "And it is armor. Not merely skin." His abdomen tightens, and he holds his breath—as I watch the surface of him change.

His skin thickens, strengthens, into something like armor. I trace the emerging diamond pattern that shines like metallic gold in the sunshine. He's so bright, it's as though the sunlight isn't glancing off of him, but rather, coming from inside him.

It's a good thing the sun is shining on him from the side, not head on, or I'd be blinded. "You're made of gold."

He smiles, and it's stunning, seeing the gleaming surface of his face bend with his curving lips. "A hundred Ssedez in the sun will blind an army on the battlefield. Alas, most of our battles are now in space, so it rarely helps."

Even his hair seems effervescent, as though laced with sunlight. It hangs in waves, brushing his shoulders, reflecting the sun the same way as his natural armor.

There's another myth that I've always wondered if it was true. The human history books deny it. "Are you the Oten who saved the Ssedez from certain genocide by piloting a star cruiser solo into the Ten Systems' fleet, destroying them by blowing up your own ship?"

His eyes go wide with surprise. "It was not solo. There were many warriors aboard. I didn't know the humans told it as a genocide tale."

"They don't. But that's what it was. They feared your immortality."

He nods. "And our honor."

"How did you survive it?"

He straightens his shoulders. "Why would I reveal such a secret to you? You are one of them."

I don't correct him. It won't matter to him that I left the Ten Systems' fleet and commandeered a ship with a crew who believe the same as me: the conquer-or-be-conquered Ten Systems' treatise is unethical. I am human. My ancestors sought to destroy his species and believe they succeeded. He has every right to hate me.

He is not god*like*—he *is* an immortal.

Whose cock stands at attention, sheathed in leather, before my eyes.

My military agenda becomes meaningless in the resurfacing of my lifelong fascination with Oten, the Sun God, and his son of the same name. The long repression of my sexuality is over. I have no reason left not to suck his cock.

He tenses, and his armor recedes. The diamond pattern merges back into his skin, leaving it smooth again. Almost like human skin, still gold, just without the shiny metallic hue.

I run my hands across his abs, feeling the texture of him.

He's hard to the touch.

I pull at the laces of his leathers, and what's exposed is as godlike as I'd hoped it would be.

Long and thick—if I thought the rest of him was hard, his cock is marble. Except it's not smooth like the rest of his skin without the armor. He's ribbed. There's a spiral pattern of ridges along his cock. They wrap around him and swirl from base to tip. The apex is a seam, the only one on his body.

I rasp, in awe. "Does it feel?"

He grunts an affirmative. "What are you going to do?"

I grasp him with my hand, my fingers not able to meet around his impressive girth. He steals a hard breath through his teeth, and his hips buck. He braces his hands on my shoulders.

"It burns, doesn't it?" I ask him.

He nods, his breath ragged. "Like a fire raging through my veins."

"I can help." I slide my hand up and down him. His ridges tickle my palm. And I have to know what he feels like in my mouth.

Chapter Six

OTEN

Her little hand around my cock—the softness of her delicate human skin.

Heat pours into my blood. The pain of it is taking over me. Either she helps me, or I help myself, but I am going to come soon whether I want to or not. She is licking her lips though, staring at me.

"General Nem," I say. "Are you going to worship an immortal Ssedez with your mouth?" I am not immortal, long-lifed yes, but killable. Our immortality is a myth we let the humans believe. She does not need to know the truth. Her ignorance and reverence are my advantage.

"Worship, no," she growls, her voice raked with an animal desire. "But I will suck you off."

I cannot think why she would want to do this. I do know that seeing her, I want nothing more. A possessiveness stiffens in my chest: *She is mine, and she knows it.*

No. I know this is not true, no matter how much my body

tells me. The physical drive within me that is confusing her for my mate is a lie. Fyrian is fucking with my system. She is as much my enemy as she was on her ship.

Except I cannot kill her now, because I need her to survive, to ease the excruciating burn for sex this place floods into my veins. It is convenient that she does not repulse me in any way, that her attractive form and aggressive demeanor are inexplicable turn-ons for me.

When she fell to her knees in sexual agony, I was helpless not to satisfy her. Feeling her coming around my fingers—her wetness—I have never felt that before. Ssedez females do not secrete.

Perhaps it is only a symptom of this place, but it is utterly erotic. It made me ache to know what it would be like to slip my cock inside her—and slide in and out, hard and fast. The friction would be a divine pleasure.

"You think to make amends for the human crimes against the Ssedez?" There is no other reason why she would do this.

"No. You killed my crew. I make no amends."

"Then why?" The flames lick hot inside me. I do not know where I have found this restraint to ask her.

Mischief streams hot from her eyes. "I want to know what a gold cock tastes like."

My brows go up. Surprise, the general has a sense of humor. "Then open and find out." I run a finger down her jaw.

She places me on her tongue, and the warmth of that small touch is stronger than any of the fire raging in me. Her lips wrap me, and a loud groan escapes me.

I am gone.

A chuckle from her throat vibrates into me, and she takes more of me into her mouth. My fangs ache. They are perma-extended, as unable to retract as my cock is to soften. The venom pools in my mouth, and the need to bite her is as strong as the one to lay her out and fuck her.

She descends, and my cock disappears inside her mouth. Though not all. There's too much of me for all.

I cannot bite her again. Injecting my enemy with the venom meant only for a Ssedez mate is sacrilege—and it was a deplorable mistake. I have no idea what more of it will do to her. Once did nothing so far, but a second time…

She does something with her tongue. I see it move behind her hollowed cheeks, and I grasp her head. I pause her movements. I cannot take it. I will spill in her mouth. Which is not an option. The Ssedez seed is only potent when the venom is flowing, and it does more than procreate with one's mate.

But she sucks on me, her throat working, and I can't resist anymore. The need in me is too great to stop her, the fire too demanding.

The ridges covering my cock rub over her lips and tongue as she moves me. The thick covering at the tip pulls back inside her mouth, exposing my most vulnerable place, my Achilles heel. That I am opening this up to her—a human who is out to kill me—is a sign of how far gone I am. It must be the Attachment, or maybe this place. Otherwise, I would never do this. I think.

I come and pour into her what I should never give her, what no Ssedez has ever given a human. I have no idea what it will do to her.

But the need to climax, the need to make her mine, overpowers any desire I have to pull out of her mouth. The orgasm rips through me, enflaming the burn, torching my nerves.

She starts to shudder and moan around my cock in her mouth, like she's about to climax.

I see her hand between her legs. She is pleasuring herself. I like this very much.

She cries out, barely audible, still sucking on my cock. The arousal doesn't soften. In fact, I bend to grab her shoulders. I want to throw her down, spread her legs, and fuck her.

But no. I stop myself.

If I do that, I will bite her again. And that cannot happen.

I pull my cock from her mouth and watch the covering of ridges curl back into place over the vulnerable tip.

"It's like foreskin," she says in fascination.

I lace up my leathers. I don't need her dwelling on that particular part of me any more than she has to. She has no idea that she's found the one and only weakness on my body, the only penetrable part of me. "It is like the Ssedez."

"I mean—"

"Do not compare me to your species," I snap. To be likened to her foul, loathsome kind, those murderers and torturers with no morality or honor, is the ultimate insult.

She stands and gives me a hard look. I expect a retort, but none comes. I should kill her now, just for saying that. The anger seethes in my chest.

But my hands do not tense. I am incapable of a violent attack toward her, not while my body believes she is destined to be my mate for life.

She searches for her weapons belt, which one of us removed at some point, though I do not remember. She retrieves it and buckles it on. She checks the computer, finds my knife she dropped, and continues on her trek through the jungle.

"Come on, Oten," she calls over her shoulder. "We've got tracks to make before this fire shit gets us again."

I grab the pack of survival gear.

She's right, I realize. We've sated the fire, but it's only simmering within me. It will blaze again and soon.

If it's going to be this way the entire time we are on forsaken Fyrian, I do not know how I am to hold anything back from her.

She could own my heart and soul before this is over.

Impossible.

I will die before I let that happen.

Chapter Seven

Nem

He follows me. But I ignore him.

I cut through the undergrowth with a vengeance. The vegetation is a predator in this place. The spines and thorns jutting from the various plants are more toxic than the air. I begin to recognize them. The darker bluer ones are the worst—with their spines like barbs that tear as well as slice my skin.

The green plants merely cut. The purple ones stab. And the trees, well, their branches are high enough, sweeping overhead and blocking the sun, so I hopefully will never find out.

I will not let these plants infect me with their sex-inducing poison anymore. I can resist him.

I must resist him.

We could come across an escape pod from my ship any moment. The locator signal could be broken. I focus hard on that—the hope of recovering my crew. I dwell on the names of my dead, at least those I know of, and I pray for them. I pray for the ones I hope were spared. I haven't prayed since I was a child, but it focuses my mind.

Mostly.

Oten walks behind me. The spawn of *the* Oten, who is at very least a demi-god.

And I sucked his cock.

The memory thickens the lust in my veins. The tip of his cock opened when he orgasmed and exposed the most vulnerable flesh. More tender than my human skin. His come spilling over my tongue wasn't sweet. No. But it was thick and satisfying. It was meaty somehow, like it had a substance to it. It coated my throat, and I can feel it in my belly, doing something, as though it's giving me strength, energy.

I won't complain about that.

The jungle is no match for me.

And even Oten can't deter me.

"How did you get aboard my ship?" I ask, not looking over my shoulder at him. Though I hear him following me. "And don't say the traitor thing again. I know it's a lie."

"How can you be sure?"

"Because no one on my crew would betray me." I know each of them well and personally.

"Denial is not an effective trait in a leader."

"Even if there were a traitor, how did he smuggle you onto my ship?"

"Are you the only female soldier among your numbers?"

"No." I know of one other who revealed herself to me and me alone. Though I did not reveal myself to her. "We don't expose ourselves."

"But how do you know if you do not expose yourselves?"

"I had one ask me to repeal the single-gender regulation when—" Do I want to tell him we went rogue from the rest of the fleet? The Ten Systems believe our ship disappeared. I'd rather keep it that way. "I refused her."

"Why? A female should be free to be herself."

"Like you said, to be treasured like glass, right? She is fragile and an object," I say with bitter sarcasm.

"I did not say that she is fragile. She is a treasure because she is valuable for her skills that males do not have."

I falter in my step, and a leaf cuts me. Damn it. "What skills do your Ssedez female warriors possess?"

"They make great leaders. Many have a stronger ability to negotiate and see from others' points of view. They can resolve disagreements better than males. They can often better predict the moves of the enemy for the same reason."

He's right. I've often thought this about human women, though most human men do not understand it. "Your male warriors aren't intimidated by a woman who can predict a situation better than they can?" I seriously doubt that.

"They are grateful for those who can see and help in ways they cannot."

Sounds like I should've been born a Ssedez. Though I won't tell him that. "It doesn't matter. Hiding our sex solves more problems than it causes." I could've abolished the rule aboard my ship, but another reason I did not was that my whole crew was so used to it. I didn't want to cause any more shake-up than I already had.

"And when and if we find your crew, how will they recognize you?"

My heart beats a little faster. I hadn't thought of that.

"Without your armor with your credentials on it," he continues, "will they believe you are their general?"

I'd left all my identification behind. Everything that denotes my rank. I trust my crew, but I don't know how far they'll trust me. I can't respond.

I consider it, but we've come too far to go back. It would add hours to our trip. But the fear he's inspired is there. I don't know if my crew will recognize me.

I hate him for spotting my weakness. I'm mad at myself for not thinking of it.

I'm the general of my mission, for fuck's sake. If I can't keep my shit together, I shouldn't be in charge. I'm smarter than this. Getting marooned on a planet with the enemy, having lost my ship, the priceless research aboard, and likely most of my crew—it is an inexcusable series of mistakes I would never have made, if not for him.

I fantasize about ways I could kill him.

I wonder if cutting off his cock would work, while he's unaware and his natural armor is not out. I wonder how fast he can…pull it out or whatever he does to put on his protective skin armor.

We travel on, mile after mile. The burning returns, and, in an effort to quench it, we consume the supply of water in the survival pack. The sweat pours off of me. The heat is so intense, we drain our three-day supply in twelve hours. We eat the dried food, but the heat exhaustion makes it difficult to digest.

Our pace slows, both of our breathing labored.

The hallucinations have returned, which are so much worse now that I actually know what his cock looks like. I keep wanting to see it, thrusting between my legs. To feel the ridges along his length sliding across my sensitive, swollen flesh. To have him rubbing inside me over and over and over…I ache for it.

It does not help that every time I turn around, I see his fangs and cock are perpetually extended. I wonder why he didn't bite me the last time. I want him to.

"Why can't you go without water, O Immortal One?" I accuse him, trying to find any excuse to ignore the mental images.

"I normally can for a very long time. On Fyrian, it

appears not." His voice rumbles low and sends more bolts of arousal straight to my enflamed flesh. I stopped trying to rub it between steps; trying to ease it made it worse.

We hear a stream, and the sound of the water is like an aphrodisiac. We move faster.

Oten moves ahead of me. "I will try it first. To see if it is safe."

"I can test it," I murmur. "There's a filter in the pack."

But either I'm too quiet or he's too desperate, because he ignores me. He goes straight to the water's edge and dunks his face in.

I manage to hold back, enduring my thirst and the fire within me. I stare at his back, the rippling muscle seeming to glow, the sunlight caressing his gold flesh.

He kneels back from the water's edge and wipes his mouth. "It's fine. Drink it." But the moment the words come out of his mouth, his hands start to shake.

The movement bleeds down his arms and into his torso until his whole body is convulsing. He moans in pain and falls to his back.

"Oten, what's wrong?" I rush to his side, but it's too obvious. He's having what looks like a seizure, and I worry he's been poisoned.

His quaking hands move down his body, wiping at his skin as though trying to put out the flames. His hands vibrate lower, yanking open his leathers, and go straight for his cock.

He grasps it and starts stroking—more like pulling on it—so hard it has to hurt.

It's the desire toxin doing this to him. It must be concentrated in the water.

"Stop. I'll help." I pull off my weapons belt and unzip my suit from the neck down. Seeing him jerking himself like that feeds the lust searing through me.

He sees me, the open zipper baring my chest. And it does

what I'd hoped. He detaches one hand from his cock and latches onto my breast. He squeezes, and it should hurt, but I ache so much, the pressure relieves it.

His jaw works as though trying to bite the air. Some liquid drips from his fangs, and the memory of the ecstasy from the last time he put them in me is too strong to ignore.

I lift his head and order, "Bite me."

His gaze is unflinching over my breasts, and he shows no reaction. He can't understand me. So I show him.

I lower my neck in front of his face, blocking his vision of my chest and exposing my throat. It works.

He grasps me with both hands and strikes. His fangs penetrate, and the effect is instant.

Euphoria pours through me. It renders me useless, claims my senses, and steals my control. It is bliss. The sting of his bite mixes with the pleasure.

My body tenses and pulses, orgasmic waves racing up and down my spine.

My empty core clenches on nothing, and I beg, "Fuck me, fuck me. Please."

Either he hears me, or that's all he wants, too. He rips my suit open through the groin, tearing the seams, then tosses me onto my back.

I hold his head to my neck, not allowing his fangs to retract, addicted to his bite.

He spreads my legs around his hips, and, without any hesitation, drives his cock into me.

I cry out, his invasion both a filling and a taking. He's so full inside me, stretching me to the brink in stinging bliss, I come around him, gripping the hardness of him. He grinds into me, pressing as deep as he can go, but then he shifts and pulls out.

His thrust back in is punishing—punishing with pleasure. The ridges on his cock are as good as I knew they'd be, better.

They rub at me in all the perfect places. His hips pound against mine over and over. The spirals around his cock ripple into me on each entry—like he's spinning through me.

The pleasure is so much, too much. More than I can take. I enter a state of mindlessness. So overcome by the sensations he gives me, I am only that ecstasy. Only that bliss. And there is only him.

He lets go his bite, leaning on his arms over me, and I watch him.

The unyielding planes of his chest bulge and contract. I grip his arms, digging my fingers into the impenetrable surface. The sharp cut to his jaw, the fierce length of his fangs, and his eyes…

They're possessed by an ethereal glow, boring into me. His almost human qualities are gone, and what's exposed is the merciless carnality.

He lets out a brutal cry of release and comes. The warmth of what he pours into me spreads through my body. It transforms on its path, filling me in all the places his cock cannot reach. A total takeover of my body.

It lasts for minutes. He comes for I don't know how long.

When he stills and quiets, the only sounds left are from our breathing. The feeling he poured into me fades.

But in its place is a vacancy.

And I want him again.

Chapter Eight

OTEN

She makes me feel…powerful. Sex for me—with me—is always that way.

I do nothing without the full experience of what I am, and I am as fierce in passion as I am in battle.

But this…

The water I drank was a drug, but I did not know it until too late.

The fire I thought I experienced before was nothing compared to this. It rages on a path of destruction, wrecking all in me that is conscious, leaving behind only carnal instinct.

She is there. She offers herself to me, and I have to have her.

She comes as she must before I can enter her, her body primed by my venom for the sex I will give her. The wetness that flows between her legs is an anomaly for me. It paves the way for my cock and lets me move in and out of her faster than I have known.

It is new to me.

She begs for me to fuck her.

I will not deny her.

Her cunt is the softest haven there is. Not just because it is unique to me, but because it is *her*. This being who is the new source of all the desire storming within me—I am compelled by the need to mark her so she and everyone knows it.

The venom and my come combine within her, and the scent of it emanates from her pores.

She smells like me. As though she's mine.

This reaction I have to her, it could be because of the water and this chemical that Fyrian produces to intoxicate us. But even if it is caused by a chemical, it doesn't change the awakened instinct in me.

Or the fact that once is not enough.

But she lies sated and slack. She cannot take more.

I pull out of her and see the thick fluids I poured into her dripping out onto her swollen folds. I want them to stay in her, so I urge her thighs closed.

But she moans, "No," and reaches down between her legs. She massages herself as though she is still needy. She soaks her fingers in the come at her opening and raises dripping fingers to her lips, leaving a trail across her belly on the way.

Her pink tongue licks her fingers clean, then she looks at me with hungry eyes. "More."

I draw in a sharp breath. My cock pulses and jerks. "I will give it."

Except this time, I have some sense.

I strip off my chest holsters, marveling that I did not injure her with my knives the first time. I want to strip her; I want us both naked. I want to feel her skin against mine. But I will not fuck her in the dirt again.

I find the pack of survival gear and pull out the ground covering.

She whimpers. "Oten…" The need in her voice is heavy, and she rolls to her side, her thighs pinched together around her hands massaging herself.

"I am here."

"Come back."

"Soon." Between me and this place, the unconquerable General Nem has become sex crazed. After who knows how long that she has been pretending to be male. Anger seethes within me at the thought of her having to hide her femininity. She deserves this pleasure. Her body needs this.

I have a thought that caring for her like this is contrary to the hatred I feel for her and her kind. But it does not matter. Now that I have had her, now that she is marked as mine, I will treat her as such. There is no sense to it. Only instinct.

I lay her on the ground cover, and she lets me undress her. I savor the feel of her skin, and she responds to my hands. So soft, so vulnerable, so giving. I strip her of her clothing that is in tatters from my ripping the zipper and from the cuts of the jungle plants. I pull off her boots and place her weapons next to her.

She is laid out and bare for me. Naked.

I must protect her.

"Now you," she murmurs, pointing at me.

There is not much for me to remove. I take off my boots and leather and stand before her, nude.

Her gaze holds fast on me. It wanders up and down my body. She squirms, writhing, and opens her legs to me. "Now."

Through force of will, I retract my fangs. I will use them again later.

I kneel between her legs and spread her thighs open. The Ssedez female must come before she will open for a male. It seems wrong for her not to come first before I fuck her again.

Besides, I want to taste her.

I press my mouth to her cunt, and sweet nectar of the

gods, I could drink her down.

I lick her every crevice. The twin tips of my serpent's tongue reaching into the depths of her. I stroke her and suck on her until she is arching her hips, thrusting against my mouth.

She comes, and I insert my fingers into her, feeling her spasm around them.

Unable to withhold my fangs any longer and wanting to fuel her pleasure, I let them descend and sink them into her thigh.

Screams of pleasure cascade from her mouth. She clenches around my fingers in rapid pulses, and I must feel her around my cock.

I fuck her until I come.

And then I do it all again.

And again.

There is no sating her. Or me.

In a brief moment of reason, she whispers, "I need to get to my ship."

By then, the sun is descending behind the hills, and travel will be difficult in the dusk light. "It will be dark soon."

She barely hears my answer. She is already at my cock, sucking on me for more.

I worry what I have done to her, what this place has done to us. I do not know what too much sex can do to a human, especially too much sex with a Ssedez. But when the sun disappears, the giant star's light gone, the fire lessens.

Her breathing returns to normal. "Is it...has it stopped?" she asks, her voice more lucid than it's been in hours.

I check my own body and find the unnatural flames that have raged within me since landing in the pod have retreated. Not gone, but they are a murmur. "It feels less. More tolerable."

"It must be activated by the sun's heat." She sits up, though

I am unable to see her. There is little moonlight. "There are headlamps in the survival gear. We can travel."

But even as she says it, there's a fatigue in her tone.

And I am low on energy as well. "We should rest for a few hours, then maybe get up before the sun rises."

She agrees wordlessly and lies down next to me. "We can't let this happen again tomorrow. We have to keep moving."

"I am motivated to get off Fyrian. We will find a way." Though if we find her crew, they will likely try to kill me. But not if I kill them first. Not if I communicate with my warriors from the wreckage of her ship and they join me on this planet so we can complete our mission to destroy Nem and any other survivors from her crew.

But I listen to her breathing slow as she drifts to sleep.

And there is a resistance in me to all my thoughts of conquering her. It is a realization of horror.

My physical Attachment to her, it has cemented in my gut like the endless sands of time. It believes she is physically a part of me that I could no more cut off than my own hand.

But I still have my reason. I have not lost my mind or my emotions to her yet.

I have to overcome this repulsive Attachment to her the sex created.

I cannot be a slave to her or my physical desire.

Chapter Nine

Nem

The relief from the flames sends me into a dreamful sleep—filled with visions of my gold alien god. In my dreams, he fucks me every way a woman can be fucked.

And then when night falls, he sleeps beside me, not touching me, but he's such a formidable presence, I can feel him as though he's surrounding me.

And there is a comfort there.

His care in my pleasure was…confusing. This situation could so easily be about us using each other to get off. But my concern for his pain when he was poisoned by the water was…astonishing. Something more than mere lust is happening between us.

This place is wreaking more havoc on us than just desire. It's as though it's making us care about the other's needs. Maybe it's just because the sex is literally so fucking otherworldly.

I sleep, twisting with anxiety, worried for my crew,

ashamed of my weakness.

I dream of chasing Oten, intending to kill him, poised to strike, then ending up beneath him instead, his cock relentlessly pounding me full of orgasms, ceaselessly.

I dream of kissing him, sucking on his tongue, then feeling his fangs prick my lips and tasting his syrupy sweet venom.

But there's another dream of horror that wakes me. A dozen Ssedez massacring my entire crew—all of my soldiers' bloody bodies on the ground—their helms pulled off and me seeing their faces for the first time, dead.

The morning light sprinkles through the trees, and I am alone.

The bed he made us is empty.

The desirous flames aren't back yet, and I'm grateful for a break from them and him. I've never had so much sex at one time in my life.

And yet, I know as surely as I need to breathe, I'll want more.

Even as I'm shaking from the terrible dream and what I know he and his warriors attempted against my crew, I'm still craving him.

I feel different. My body is stronger, sturdier, my limbs more lithe. So it's not like sex with him has been bad for me.

But then I touch my arm, and something else is different.

I look down at my naked form, and my heart speeds. "No!"

I run my hands over myself, disbelieving. It can't be real. It must be more hallucinations. I've started seeing things even on myself.

But I pick up one of his knives next to me and prick my forearm.

It leaves a scratch. But it doesn't cut me. I slice the blade over my skin again and again, willing it to draw blood, screaming at it to harm me. But nothing happens.

The sun lifts, the rays spreading onto my legs—that aren't pale anymore.

They gleam, as though turned to gold. Like his.

He's made me like him.

Shock seizes me—what I've done, what he's done. I never suspected... If I had known...would I have stopped him? Would I have been able to drum up the restraint to say no?

The memory of the pain and flames raging through my blood is still vivid.

I couldn't have resisted him. Not when the relief he brought was so complete and ecstatic.

He just had to be capable of transforming a human into himself. Did he know this would happen? Was using his sex and his venom on me as much a weapon as any knife or blaster?

Is the change permanent?

My skin has a new texture. It's thicker, more durable. It's still smooth, if not smoother than my own, and still soft in a different way, but now there are tiny sparkles across the surface. I glisten.

A dull ache throbs in my upper jaw. I finger my teeth and find a new set of incisors probing my gums.

I pull forward a piece of my hair and find it run with gold strands, though some are still brunette.

I've never heard of this. Never in any of my grandmother Dr. Eda Klearuh's research did I hear of interspecies sex causing a change of one's cellular makeup.

I've memorized her theories on the common marks of all intelligent life in the universe. I've been riveted by her theories. After evolution and the "big bang" theories were proved correct, she set out to prove all intelligent life in the universe stems from the same source. Her discoveries ran contrary to the Ten Systems' credo, which is that humans are the dominant beings destined to rule all others.

My parents died protecting her research, hiding it where only their daughter knew where to find it. The military forces the best scientists into service for their own agenda to prove one and only one thing: humans are the superior species, ordained by nature to conquer. I was raised with the knowledge that only by infiltrating the Ten Systems' military could I learn their tactics well enough to extract key scientists, evade the authorities, and escape.

I recruited as many as I could who believed what Dr. Klearuh's studies, if completed, will likely prove: all intelligent life, in every galaxy, in any form, is equal.

We escaped with the best crew we could find with the sole goal of rebellion against the Ten Systems to continue her work.

But I failed in my mission. Dr. Klearuh's findings, the cause my parents died for and my crew risked their lives for, is gone.

All the files were likely destroyed along with my ship. Unless someone else in the crew managed to save it and survive.

Oten.

He's the reason for all of this.

His fluids worked a transformation on me. Whether it is from his venom or his semen, I don't know. But I do know I can't let him put any of his liquid in me again.

The changes can't be permanent. They'll pass through my system like any other injections would. They have to.

How this rapid change is scientifically possible, I don't know.

I read no notes on the Ssedez and their evolution in my grandmother's research. There was so much information she'd gathered from dozens of ships and thousands of scientists, I couldn't read it all. Those in my crew combined may have combed through it, though they wouldn't have memorized it.

Gone. All that precious knowledge.

Because of him.

Rage builds in me like a coming explosion. It ricochets inside my skull with the force of split atoms in a reactor. I can't let him beat me.

He will pay.

"Oten!" Wherever the fuck he is. I've let my guard down with him. He's probably still planning to kill me. I can't let that happen. I can't let him win.

Chapter Ten

Oten

I watch her from amidst a copse of bushes.

I am not a coward. I am shocked.

She needs space—I need space—to comprehend what I have done to her. I predicted it would be something, before I lost my mind to the madness of this hellish planet and its damned sun.

But I never thought it would be this.

The dawn revealed her change. I did not know it would happen. I swear, I would have found a way to resist her had I known. To change her, to force a transformation on her, is fundamentally wrong, no matter how much I like it.

I should feel guilt at her skin turning the tone and texture of mine. The armored quality she now has should be a bad thing. She will be harder to kill.

Disgust at seeing her—a human—transform into a Ssedez would be a reasonable reaction.

But I cannot think or feel any of those things.

Instead, I feel a satisfaction as deep as the fires burning within the largest star of the brightest solar system. I know beyond doubt—

She is mine.

She is genetically laced with parts of me.

I have made her stronger. I have given her protection.

She will need exterior armor no longer.

She now *is* armor. My armor.

Pride breeds in my chest with the power of my life's blood. To see her—the female my body has physically Attached to—turn Ssedez makes me want to boom the news of it from the treetops. I want everyone to see her this way. I want everyone—from this galaxy and beyond—to know she belongs to me.

I want them to witness I did that to her, with my sex and my bite.

The strength of my response is—horrifying. If I could sever this Attachment from my body, I would. If I could cut her out of me, no matter what the pain, I would carve the hole in myself with my own knives.

I cannot be feeling this for a human. I cannot. It should be impossible.

But no matter how unwilling my reason, I cannot control the instinct.

My heart, my soul seethe with emptiness. I have longed for this—for my body to feel this for another Ssedez—for a hundred years. I have in vain sought a mate and never found one who called to my instincts the way this human does.

That the Attachment should awaken in me now, for her, is painful, and a mockery of my heart's desire.

It is because of this place.

I tell myself again, *My feelings are not real.*

My body does not understand this truth. It only knows what it craves.

That she is mine to the point of changing her cellular

makeup affects me on an instinctual level.

But it does not make it right.

It is hopefully temporary and will pass from her system. If I do not give her more of me.

The need to infect her further, to make it permanent, beats through my blood and rises through my cock. It should be aching from overuse, but it is not.

My body is made for the mating frenzy that comes with the completion of the Attachment. When my heart and soul join with my body's desire, when my emotional Attachment is equal to the physical, her life will become more important than my own. When her fangs descend for me and she returns my bite, then it will be complete. Then my lust will be even more unslakable than even Fyrian has made me. I have witnessed it among my other warriors. At the onset of the Attachment, they must be excused from duty for a week or more.

A female Ssedez is genetically able to withstand the male frenzy and return it.

This human—I doubt could withstand it. My frenzy would likely kill her.

But it will never happen because the rest of me will never Attach to her emotionally the way my body has physically. So I do not need to worry.

My gums pulse where my fangs are once more dripping with my venom. The craving to bite her has not lessened since I drank the cursed water from the stream.

I found edible fruit hanging from a tree, which I tested and found negative for toxins. I bite into one. It does not dull the ache, but it relieves some of the pressure to pour the venom into something.

Before I go near her again, I must relieve some of this accursed lust taking over my body. She is a forsaken human! I cannot be feeling these false things for her and filling her with the sacred venom, which should be reserved for my fellow Ssedez.

Procreation for us has been of paramount importance since the attempted genocide by the humans. We are still not returned to our former numbers. It has been the shame of my existence that I have not been able to father children yet.

That, mixed with the pride of claiming her, is a lethal concoction of confusion, like the most potent poison. It conjures in me an outrage and a certainty that—

I cannot give her more of myself.

No matter the compulsion of this place, I must find another way to ease the burning pain that has increased again since dawn.

I pull and squeeze at my cock as I watch her. I try to make it hurt. I need to teach it to not crave her like I need her to survive. She sits naked on the makeshift bed, her breasts in full view. I cannot help remembering the tight muscles of her ass and how they looked and felt from me fucking her countless times. So firm and yet her skin so soft.

That softness is no more. Now it will feel like mine.

It raises the pleasure in me, the orgasm building stronger.

I clamp down on the fruit in my mouth and stifle a climactic groan so she cannot hear. I watch the silver semen pump from my cock—the ridges pulled back to reveal the vulnerable tip.

But as though she can hear me, though I know I was soundless, she calls my name.

"Oten!" The anger in her tone is like a demanding beast—one that hardens my cock again, despite my orgasm. If the evidence of it were not in a shining silver puddle on the ground, I would think it never happened.

I groan, not attempting to hide it this time.

Her gaze whips to mine, and I move through the bushes.

"You're watching me?" she seethes, her mouth twisting in revulsion.

She hates me. As well she should.

I stop, away from her. I don't want to get close to her. To tempt me into touching her. To tempt her into attempting to kill me again.

Though I hope she does. I want her to attack me. To see her unleash all the anger screaming at me from her eyes, hot and murderous. I would enjoy crossing blades with her.

And then fucking her when we're done.

Which I cannot do, so fighting is not an option.

"Answer me, you fucker!" she yells, and stands. "How do you explain *thisss*?" Her tongue has changed. She hisses like a newly born Ssedez.

She gestures to her naked body of shimmering gold. My skin tone is a richer gold, while hers is lighter, as though younger and touched by the sun.

She is sensational to look upon. I peel my eyes away from the chiseled form of her warrior's body, combined with the new gleam of her—to look away is impossible. I cannot not stare at her.

I try to speak evenly, as much as I can with my cock pulsing and fangs aching. "I did not know the effect I would have on you."

"Bullshit!"

"There is no precedent for the Ssedez having relations with a human. I swear, I did not know."

"You knew it would affect me *sss*omehow," she hisses.

I see her tongue lick out, the twin tips snaking over her lips.

It makes me harder, to think of that tongue licking over my skin, of sucking it into my mouth, of her wrapping it around my cock.

I will not point it out. "I did know I would have some effect. I did not know it would change you."

She stalks toward me. "You could have warned me."

"I was not in my right mind."

"What does the venom do to the *Sssss*edez?" Her tongue lingers over the first part of our name, the correct way to say it. I have to suppress a groan. I like it.

"For the Ssedez, the venom increases sexual pleasure. Brings greater heights of ecstasy." I don't add that it is considered a great honor, a special treasure, when it does happen, since it flows only during the physical part of the Attachment. "I had no reason to believe it would cause a change in you."

"You could've *sss*peculated. You should've known."

"You, who demanded I bite you."

Her nostrils flare, but she does not deny it. She remembers it was the first thing she wanted when we got off the escape pod. The sight of my fangs extended made her desire it.

"I would not have bitten you otherwise." I would have found a way to resist. Some way. Any way.

"If I had known, I never would've succumbed." Her voice is tight with aggression, her body tense and coiling to spring. She is as vicious as a viper.

Her upper lip pulls back in a snarl, revealing the points of fangs poking through her upper gums. I have to close my eyes and look away. The sight of them sends a bolt of lust searing through my veins. To have her bite me...

To see her mouth overtaken with fangs, to have her spill her own venom into me, would *make* me. For her to return the venom would mean the ultimate completion of the physical Attachment.

A longing, thick and fierce, rises behind my lust. For her to feel the Attachment for me that I have begun to feel for her...

I want it with a ferocity that could shake the ground we stand on.

I turn away from her and let out a vicious yell. This cannot be happening to me!

These feelings are contrary to every longing that lives in my soul.

But it does not stop the desire from implanting itself in me.

The centuries of my loneliness compound within me. In the absence of a mate, I have consumed myself with the training of my warriors, with the protection of the Ssedez.

It does not mean the desire for a mate, the need for someone who pulls from my body the animal instinct to join for life, has ever died. Though I despaired of finding the one, I have never been able to give up hope.

And here she is. A human who, with her consent and more of my venom, I could turn into a Ssedez.

This place, this planet, taunts me with a hope I have clung to for too many decades.

The bitterness I feel is fiercer than even the lust the water induced yesterday.

"The affects might wear off," I say with a sneer. "I will not bite you again. And you may return to your former, vulnerable mortal self."

"Vulnerable?" she snaps.

"While you are Ssedez, you will not have to worry about the plants cutting you." I motion at the leaves that yesterday infected her with more lust than even the atmosphere.

"I don't need your venom to protect me!" The brutality in her tone is like a slicing knife. Her shoulders bunch, and her body vibrates with restrained violence.

She is a breath away from attacking me.

I want her to. The craving to touch her defies even my revulsion at her kind. And so, I am willing to say words that are not true. "You will never be as strong as I am."

A battle hiss, the precursor to a strike, bursts from her mouth, and she lunges for me.

She double kicks me, a one-two in the gut and the chin—too fast for me to block.

I stumble back but see her next swing. I catch her fist, flying straight at my eye. But she expects it, and her other fist slams me in the chest like a hammer.

The strength of her blows—though I knew they would be strong—is unexpected. I like it.

I twist her arm behind her back and put painful pressure on the socket, immobilizing her.

Or so I think.

With a slither of her arm and a knee to my thigh, she breaks my hold and squares off again.

"Still convinced you're stronger?" she taunts.

"Yes."

This time, a very human roar sounds from her throat, and she tackles me with full force. I am pushed back against a tree. I grab her throat intending to squeeze but am instead enthralled.

The texture of her changed skin against my palm rouses my desire as much as her fighting me. It leaves me open, and she takes the advantage.

She slugs her fist into the side of my head.

I am cool-blooded, so I will not bruise like humans do. But it still hurts.

I grab her, pull her off her feet, and turn. I slam her back against the tree, the trunk wide as a wall.

She grunts and pushes against me, both her feet on my thighs, her hands on my shoulders. She could shove me off her, but she stops.

Her eyes are a golden brown, unaffected, unchanged from yesterday. I am glad. They are full of hot things—rage, violence…desire.

Her bone structure is unchanged. Her lips look as soft and plump as yesterday. The tension in her legs eases, and I press against her, my cock thickening between her legs, feeling the heat of her there.

She is naked. The only thing separating my fucking her as hard and fast as yesterday is the thin leather of my fly. Her breath gusts in and out, her high breasts pumping up and down.

Her gaze strays to my mouth, and it is the only invitation I need.

I kiss her, devouring her. Our tongues clash. The feel of her more dexterous twin-tipped tongue tangling with mine, the clench of her thighs around my hips as the fight goes out of her, the grip of her fingers in my hair pulling me to her—

She wants me.

I do not know if it is because of this place or because it is true.

My fangs descend, and she wraps her tongue around one and begins to suck it.

It's like she's pulling bliss from me, and I swear, I will come, the sensations of her mouth are that intense. She pulls the venom out of me, relieving my swollen gums. I'm overcome by the sheer ecstasy that she, this creature fate has chosen for me, takes into her body the venom I offer her.

Except, that's exactly what she's not supposed to do.

Fuck.

I pull away from her so hard, she falls to the ground with a hard thud.

"Ow! Gah!" She rubs her back. "What the hell was that?"

I turn from her. My breath gasping and my body screaming, *Go back to her. Fuck her full of you. Change her until she is totally yours.*

Against every instinct roaring through my body, I focus on my hatred of her murderous kind and fist my hands at my sides. I growl, "You figure it out," and stalk to the fruit tree.

I do not know how I am surviving this, but I will cut my heart out before I give my venom to a human again. No matter how my body cries out in agony for her.

Chapter Eleven

Nem

He leaves, and I touch my lips, where the taste of his venom is still heavy on my tongue.

"Goddamn it!" I snarl. The tip of my tongue brushes my fingertips, and I freeze.

I touch my tongue. Before it was unwieldy, wide, and thick. Now it's razor thin and narrow with…

I hate him. I hate him so fucking much, I'd kill him now. If I could.

I didn't notice it while kissing him; all I noticed was that I felt more of his tongue. I could reach all the way into the back of his mouth, wrap my tongue around his, and pull. I could do things I hadn't done before.

The forked tips of what is now my tongue flick at my fingers. I wish to the god of anything that I had a mirror. But there's no such thing in that pack. I have to get this venom out of me.

I spit and gag myself, getting as much of what I swallowed out on the ground. I scrape my tongue with my fingers. I need water to wash out my mouth.

Except we have none. We drank it all. And that cursed stream is what caused this whole problem.

No wonder my body changed in a matter of hours. I was so pumped full of his fluids from who knows how many times having sex that if a change was going to happen, it was going to be fast.

But it's been such a short time. Maybe it's possible to wash his toxins out of me. I'm desperate for any hope this isn't permanent.

I rush to the pack of survival supplies, not caring that I'm still naked. Like I give a shit. I'm gold now anyway. Water is more important.

I grab the bottle and filter with one hand and the testing computer with the other and head for the stream.

He better not be nearby. I won't touch him again, not even to hit him. I can't shoot him because the blaster fueled him rather than injured him. Knives will just bounce off of him.

I have to figure out how to get rid of him.

Water first. I hope he's off somewhere jerking off again, or finding something else to bite instead of me.

The stream bank is covered in vegetation, but the leaves only scratch me. I grumble under my breath and refuse to feel gratitude for my new natural armor.

The water flows slowly and is warm to the touch, but it's clear and moving. I test a sample in the computer, and it contains no bacteria—only large quantities of the compound unique to this planet that permeates the air and causes this fever of desire, which even now I'm feeling rise in me again.

I fill the bottle with the clear liquid, then place the filter top on and wait.

The lasers in the filter light up the water a bright iridescent red. The filter excretes a dusty red residue, what I can only assume is the deposits of the desire compound.

I test the filtered water. Which is now 99 percent pure. Good enough.

I drink, first rinsing my mouth and spitting, then swallowing the rest. I filter and drink a second bottle, then fill a third to take with me.

I gather up the ground covering and blankets, forcing everything into the pack.

My white skin suit lies in a heap of tatters on the ground. I have no desire to put it on. But to go naked feels too barbaric. I may not need it for protection now, but if my skin does return to normal, I'll want it. I wrap what's left of the suit around my waist. It covers my ass and groin if nothing else. I buckle my weapons belt with my blaster over the top and pull on my boots.

I look down at my breasts. My nipples are now gold jewel-like points, still sensitive though, and with the heat of the day rising, the dull flames have returned to my veins.

I don't know where Oten is. I'm ready to leave. I want to make progress before the sun gets higher and the feeling gets worse. I can't be near him when it comes back. My own hand is my only source of relief now.

He doesn't have water.

I shouldn't care. I want him dead. He killed my crew. Destroyed my ship. Turned me into another species.

But for some reason, I can't leave him without water.

I fill another bottle with filtered water and set it on the ground where our bed was. He can't miss it.

I do it because I don't want him to die of thirst—I want to kill him myself. That's what I tell myself.

My ship, the surviving members of my crew, and Dr. Klearuh's research are my goal. I have to find them. No orgasms from an enormous gold cock or fangs dripping in ecstasy will distract me today.

But it can't stop me from thinking about them every step I take.

Chapter Twelve

Oten

When I gain control of myself and go back, Nem is gone.

I am glad.

She left my chest holsters with my weapons, which could be a peace offering, but I am not fooled. It is a challenge. My knives will have no effect on her now. I will need other weapons if I am to defeat her.

I could have choked her so easily, cut off her air and watched her suffocate.

It would have been apt justice. What her human Ten Systems did to the Ssedez in our war over a century ago was so much worse—destroying civilian cruisers, mass killing of children and families. While our armored skin is impervious to most weapons, strong fire and exposure to the vacuum of space will kill us.

But even though my hand was around her throat, I could not kill her.

I am forced to admit defeat to my own dominant instincts.

I may be in control of my emotions and my mind, but my body will not allow me to do her violence. It is too far gone with the Attachment.

I do not have the will to hurt her.

I do have the will to fuck her. I have to stay away from her. My resistance to her is brittle.

It is still within me—the anger of my existence. The craving for retaliation that has been with me since the humans first attacked a peaceful cruiser killing thousands of civilian Ssedez. When I entered the war, I was a newly trained warrior hungry to avenge the deaths of so many loved ones I lost: my father and uncle among the first battalions destroyed in the war. My aunt and cousins murdered in horrible ways I try not to contemplate.

The humans saw us as a threat—our near-immortal selves, our inexplicable technology they could not understand. They sought to do experiments on us. No one ever escaped their imprisonment. We can only speculate what was done to the captured, or if any of them may still be alive.

Decades of hostile conflict ensued, and the deaths of a million Ssedez. We made the choice—deciding we had suffered enough tragedy—to end it. We stealthily evacuated our home world and set off a series of bombs, made to look like volcanic explosions over the planet, which destroyed the ecosystems and made it uninhabitable. The humans believed it a natural destruction of our world and had no idea we had faked our demise. We annihilated our home and can never return—a decision, though necessary, that we have mourned for generations. We have maintained our isolation. Nem's ship, the *Origin*, in our airspace was the first we had seen of the Ten Systems in a century. But we were ready.

And we succeeded in bringing her down.

The ship that is.

Not her captain.

I mourn the lives of a million Ssedez, including friends and family whose places still occupy my heart, and yet I cannot end her. I am incapable of harming her. Even when she attacked me, I could only restrain her, never hit her.

I should feel shame.

Instead, I feel a need to learn her, physically. I feel a terrifyingly intense craving to satisfy every want, every desire of her body. I have to know what a human woman wants—what *this* woman wants—so that I can give it to her.

Again and again. So she will never need anything but me.

I shake myself and strap on my weapons.

It is the false physical Attachment sabotaging my thoughts and making me forget who she really is.

I should learn why her Ten Systems' ship flew stealthily into our uncharted, uninhabited system. And when we can expect other ships to follow. We must be ready.

But I am lying to myself if I think that is the only reason I am leaving her alive.

I see the bottle of water.

She left me hydration. I examine it, sniff the liquid. Not that I know what I'm searching for; my sense of smell is not one of my enhanced abilities. I have no way of sensing whether she purified it with the filter she mentioned having in the survival supplies. It could be a trick.

My instinct—though it goes against everything I've known of humans all my life—says she would not trick me.

There is honor in her. Though I never thought a human capable of it, she has it.

In her fascinations and questions about my people, there was no hatred or derision. Only curiosity. I would not have expected it from a human.

I thought them capable of only a greed for dominance and an obsession with power.

But there is more to her.

I do not think she would poison me.

Attempt to kill me, maybe. But only by her own hand.

Though after I infected her with the genes of the Ssedez, which are obviously overpowering her human ones, she is capable of anything.

I open the bottle and drink. Nothing happens, so I drink until it is gone.

I follow her path through the jungle easily. She has scales now to protect her from the sharp leaves, but she's still using my machete to cut the vegetation. The jungle thickens, the stream we found grows wider, deeper, and with it the size of the trees and plants. They are no longer just waist high, but up to my shoulders.

Her path is clear though. She made it so.

Why? She has no need to chop down the vegetation with the Ssedez armor to protect her. She must be doing it to make sure I follow her.

I force myself not to hurry, not to think about how good it was to be inside her. To feel her around my cock and see her face light up with pleasure when I filled her. To grip her flesh as I pounded her and watched her body shake as orgasms seized her.

The best part was seeing her lose it.

While I was in her, the general disappeared, and she was all female.

The sun gets higher, and the air heats. It gets blindingly bright, and I get a glimpse through the trees of a second sun rising behind the first.

Whatever cursed thing is in the atmosphere thickens. I inhale, and it lights a fire in my lungs that spreads to my veins. My cock beats with a need for relief, and I gnaw on jungle fruit to ease the ache in my upper jaw.

I follow her trail, going slow, not wanting to catch her. I observe the environment, needing to focus on what I'm seeing rather than the arousal burning through me, broiling hotter with each hour.

I glimpse mammals of various sizes skittering on the ground or climbing the trees. Animals of flight, though I'm not sure they are birds since they lack feathers, pass overhead.

The surroundings grow monotonous, the sounds of the forest, the tweets and clicks and squeaks of creatures, become lulling and predictable. Until they are not.

A roar—long and thunderous—rattles my ears.

All the animals scurry to hide, then the forest is silent.

I crouch low and scan the trees. Whatever made that noise is something large. The sound is similar to an animal from my home world. If I am right, it is a predator.

It roars again, farther away this time.

In the direction Nem is heading.

I bolt from the ground, running her trail as fast as my legs will move—which is fast.

The leaves blur, and my muscles bunch with the forward motion, my whole body in sync with its one goal: to protect its mate.

No.

My mind rejects the instinct.

But my body does not lie, and I cannot stop its reaction.

Protect her.

The roar sounds again, and I push faster, shocked that she could be so far ahead of me. She moves faster than I thought she could.

I turn a corner, dash through a set of trees, and slide to a halt.

She stands battle ready, legs braced, blaster in one hand, knife in the other, glaring in the direction the roar came from.

I open my mouth to call to her but before I can, she motions with her knife for me to shut up.

She's right. To draw attention to us would be stupid.

The jungle remains eerily silent. We wait and wait and wait some more.

The sound does not come again.

She gradually relaxes her stance. Her pack lies on the ground, and other than the tattered suit wrapped around her waist over her weapons belt, and her ankle-high boots, she is naked. Her legs are visible from calf to hip, and her nipples are pebbles and kissed with the sun's rays.

Her body is sculpted by the gods and made to be devoured by my hands. From the contours of her high breasts to the trim of her waist and chisel of her abs, from her firm thighs to her molded biceps, she is a warrior, her strength prominent in every limb and muscle.

Her body is a weapon, and I want to wield it.

I walk closer to her, but she holds up a hand for me to stop. Her glare is as brutal as any she has yet given me.

"Don't come near me," she warns, but her body, her stance says the opposite. She's leaning toward me, as though restraining herself from coming to me.

I realize too late my fangs are fully extended.

She eyes me, and the brutality in her gaze morphs to one of heated desire. I recognize the look from yesterday when she knelt before me and told me she wanted to know what a gold cock tasted like.

She will not do that now.

I will not let her do that again.

Her change into Ssedez has not reversed. If anything, it's sped. The armor on her has thickened, the diamond pattern etched into her. She willed it to happen on instinct to defend herself from the animal. Once she relaxes, the solid armor will retreat back into her skin, which will grow smooth again. But I do not think she knows how to affect that change yet.

"Do you *sss*ee what you've done to me?" Fury shakes her voice, but I can hear through the cracks: she's afraid.

I swallow. "I see."

"Are you happy? Is it exactly what you wanted? Why couldn't you just fucking kill me instead?"

It is like she took one of my knives and pierced my heart. She would rather be dead than be like me. I should not care what she thinks. But it cuts at a vulnerable place in myself I cannot name. "You are unharmed. In fact, you are better protected."

"I need no protection," she sneers. "You're just like all the others."

"What others?"

"Males in every *sss*pecies are the same. Possessed by the need to dominate. To own and make everyone and everything belong to them."

"The Ssedez—"

"Look at me!" She yells so loud a flock of flying things squawks and takes flight. "You've made me yours so much that I'm *becoming* you!" The fear in her eyes is too fierce for her to hide now.

My instinct is to shout, *You ARE mine*. I force it down. "It may still reverse itself."

"You don't know that!" she shouts at the top of her lungs. It rings through the trees. The tone of her voice is taking on the powerful resonance of the Ssedez, too.

Her anger is like a force of nature, a twisting cyclone gathering speed, readying for destruction. A compassion stirs in me. Something I never thought to feel toward a human.

"I am sorry," I say. "I never would have touched you if I had known it was going to do this to you."

She stares at me, her lip curling, revealing once more her baby fangs. "You think that helps?"

I should know: nothing I can say will make how I have violated her any better. "No."

"You are unaffected, and I may pay the price for the rest

of my life. There is no amount of sorry that can help that."

She reholsters her blaster then turns away, continuing her slashing through the forest with my knife.

Leaving me feeling like a hole has been carved in my chest.

I scratch at it—willing it to stop hurting. I feel...strange things—things a human should never make me feel: guilt, regret, a desire to make amends.

I stare at the ground, not understanding who I am becoming. She cannot be affecting my feelings. My body's Attachment to her is purely physical. My emotions are not involved in anything pertaining to *her*.

If I start to feel anything, I will lose myself to her. It is a good thing what I have done to her has made her hate me even more.

Chapter Thirteen

Nem

I can't get him out of my head.

The sight of him—those fangs extended—

I carve through the jungle with his machete, hacking out a path for myself. I'm going faster than I thought I could. I don't think about it. Like everything else about me that's been changing. I focus on—

How much I hate him.

But that just has me thinking about him and that glorious gold cock hanging between his legs.

No.

I focus on—

The work of moving through the jungle.

But that just has me thinking about my body. And how it's broiling with the desire to run back and fuck him.

I should be hot. I should be sweating. But I'm not. My blood runs cooler. Like a reptile's.

I stop once an hour for a refill of my water bottle. I've

drunk six liters of water already today. I'll drink six more before nightfall. I don't care how much I have to pee. At least that hasn't changed.

I'm going to wash that Ssedez out of my body.

I refuse to accept that I've changed into another species. I'm human, damn it. It doesn't matter that I've rebelled against the Ten Systems. I still want to be human. I still want to be myself.

Oten toyed with me yesterday—saying my crew might not recognize me without my armor. Because I'm female.

They really won't recognize me now.

I'll find some way to convince them I'm their general.

If my second and third-in-command, my lieutenant general…

My brain fails me, and I almost stumble.

I can't remember their names. The heat raging through my veins is rampant, like it's stealing my thoughts. I won't let it.

I clench my teeth harder. Force myself to think.

Cut through the brush harder and…

Assur and Jens!

Those were their names. If they survived the crash, each of them know things that only I would know. Them, I'll be able to convince I'm me.

But…I can't remember what those things are. Something about the mission and where we were going but…where were we going?

My vision starts to blur.

I must need more water. That's what's wrong. The heat. I can't think clearly. My blood is too cool. My inability to sweat is causing me exhaustion.

I refill my bottle, filter the water, and drink.

I return to the trail, my slog through the jungle. My body starts to throb with my blood pulsing heat through my veins.

I've become so accustomed to feeling swollen between my legs, so hot, so molten. A fire burns at the apex of my thighs; it spreads through my abdomen and down my legs. My core rages and burns, painfully empty.

My crew... Where I'm going... The goal I'm trying to reach... I can't remember. There is only endless jungle and the fire in me.

Beneath my skin, flames rage. My body is crying out for touch, for sensation, for feeling. The need swells even my brain. My thoughts morph and disappear.

The sun beats down on me, and the air thickens. A moisture fills the air, a fog clouding my vision and filling my lungs—hot, so hot.

I stop.

I need feeling, physical sensation.

I brush my hands over my breasts, pinching my nipples, and it brings a burst of relief so fierce I cry out. But in its place, I'm filled with more longing.

Need. I am it. It is me.

I run my hands over my new, reinforced skin. The intricacies of the new texture—smooth yet hard—fascinates my sense of touch, the pads of my fingers hypnotized by the new sensations.

And the way my skin feels. Being touched isn't the same. I'm less sensitive, yet more so at the same time. Like my skin is thicker, more of a barrier from my regular nerve endings. But there are new nerve endings at the same time. A new kind of sensation.

Like cotton brushing over feathers.

I'm cool on the surface. That's fascinating, too.

Like my skin is cooler than I am on the inside.

I realize, or don't realize, because I don't know what's happening, that my weapons, my pack, my skin suit that was tied around my waist—are all on the ground.

I kicked off my boots.

I took it all off.

I don't want anything touching me. All of it hurts or feels like too much.

I'm naked and running my hands up and down my body. I've stopped by the stream, and in the surface of the water, I see myself.

I can't see my face; it's muddled in the ripples of the stream, but I see the outline of me. I watch my hands skim my hips and thighs, watch my gold hands move over me.

That I'm seeing me is hard to believe. It's like watching someone else. Except it's not. This is me. It's a surreal out-of-body experience. I'm shocked and horrified this other being is me. But I'm awed and excited at the same time.

I like it. I like this me that is both a new me and not me at all.

This armor that is me. I'm protected and yet wearing nothing.

My fingers slip between my thighs, over the curls at the juncture. I seek into the folds surrounding my clit and almost crumble to the ground. Being touched there—I am so enflamed—it's excruciating.

But once I start touching myself there, I can't stop.

I widen my legs and sink my fingertips into the wetness that is me.

I'm so slick and open, sliding my fingers inside is like slipping through cream. I crook my fingertips against the round spot inside, and it sends a pulse of pleasure through me. My legs weaken.

I fall to my knees on the stream bank.

I'm still visible in the water, but I'm not seeing myself anymore.

I see him.

Oten.

The gleaming immortal.

And his impressive gold cock.

My mouth falls open.

The last time I was on my knees touching myself, I had him in my mouth. The spirals of his cock brushing past my lips until the tip pealed back and revealed the soft flesh beneath.

Then there was the thickness of his come spilling onto the back of my tongue, the rich taste and the satisfying feeling as I swallowed it down my throat, and it filled my stomach.

I have to thrust my hand farther up inside me—to try and fill myself.

I lie on my back and spread my legs. The climax builds, crawling up my spine, begging to be let out.

Both my hands—rubbing across my clit—pumping inside me.

I can see him in front of me. So clearly. Like he's really there.

He stares at me. The desire and the need in his eyes, watching me. Him desiring me, wishing he could have me, as I take care of myself.

I relish in the power. I am what he wants. And he can't have me.

He pulls out his cock and grasps himself—stroking up and down. I stare at his hand. At the tip of his cock as it disappears and reappears in his palm. I watch for the gold ridges to peel back and reveal the velvety tip.

It does, and my mouth works, wishing with every fiber of me that he was fucking my mouth.

I come, climaxing.

I cry out but cannot close my eyes. I have to watch him.

He groans loud and long, an animal in the jungle, and I watch his orgasm stream from the tip of his cock. Bursts of come jet on the ground except...

It's not creamy and white like I expect it to be. It's shiny and...

Silver. It lands on the ground in gleaming bursts that twinkle in the sun.

I have to stop myself from sticking my face in the dirt and licking it up—it looks so good. Like the richness of gemstones and the consistency of the thickest sugar. As though just tasting it would be a shot of sweet ecstasy.

I moan in sadness at the waste. That should be in my mouth or between my legs.

I hunger for it. To feel it on my skin. To touch it and run my fingers through it as I paint myself with it.

My body hums with my orgasm, but I still need him.

I get on my hands and knees and crawl to him.

Chapter Fourteen

Oten

She crawls toward me, and there is enough rationale left in my deluded mind to remember that is not good.

I retreat from her.

She moves, her body curving and flexing, her eyes stalking me. She is a fierce feline, and I am her prey.

I back into a tree and hold up my hand. "Stop." I try to say it, but it comes out a whisper.

She reaches me and grabs my legs. She walks her hands up my body and stands, rubbing herself against me like a cat in heat—a lethally dangerous cat.

She caresses my abs and chest then fingers my knives. "Do you want me to stop?" she taunts.

My mind is gone. If there is a world outside of her and this explosive, consuming desire I have for her, I do not know it. I have no care in the world except her.

There is only this female.

This woman.

And my need for her.

And her need for me.

Or at least, her need for sex that has her coming to me.

I want to meet her need. To give her everything she craves with her body and her soul.

She seeks my lips with hers. I ache to kiss her.

But there is a reason—I do not remember what is it—some life-and-death reason why I should not. I cannot kiss her and let her suck on my fangs the way they are throbbing and begging to be sucked.

I grasp her shoulders and turn her before her mouth meets mine. I want to press my chest to her back, but I have to strip off my weapons first.

Before I can unbuckle my holster though, she shakes herself and jumps away from me.

"What…the…fu—" I think she means to swear but fails to finish the sentence and grasps her head like it hurts. She turns to look at me, and the expression on her face is pure horror.

I know why she is afraid. Or I think I do.

It is because we agreed not to do this. I should not be undressing or watching her make herself come. She should not be seducing me with her eyes or touching me.

But…why?

Why not?

We want each other.

Her body is crying out for sex with me as mine is for her.

There is nothing to stop us. Nothing in all the cosmos could lessen the desire between us.

But the fear in her eyes.

And the barrier in me. Some reason why I cannot have her.

I obey it.

She backs away but seems to grow weak and sinks to

the ground. I back away, too, but stay where I can see her. I cannot bring myself to leave her out of my sight. She stares at me.

The horror on her face morphs to confusion. Like she is at a loss for what is happening.

If her mind is drowning in the need to fuck, as mine is, we need to be as far away from each other as we can bear.

I sit away from the stream, my back against a tree. My body seethes with the pain of needing to bury my cock inside her. To go make her come with me imbedded in her cunt, driving into her until she grips my cock like a fist with her orgasm.

I dare not move. If I move, I will go to her.

She sits immobile, leaning against a rock.

The heat of the day swirls around us. A mist drifts over the leaves on its way to the trickling stream.

I do not know how much time passes.

Spots cloud my vision. I still see her but only her. I don't know how long we sit staring at each other. Her nakedness is a thing of beauty I am incapable of looking away from. I watch her breasts rise and fall with her breath, her long muscled legs stretched in front of her.

She opens them and stares at me while she strokes through her wet folds.

She glistens, the flesh within so swollen, so dripping, it calls to me. To be inside her, to taste her would be a trip into an erotic heaven. To sink deep within her once would not be enough. I would do it again and again until I was so far up inside her, I'd pull the screams from her throat.

I am hot, my skin oversensitive as though heat runs over me. I cannot stand the feel of my clothes or having my body confined, so I strip off my holsters and pants.

She stares at my cock lying hard and thick against my thigh. Her lips part, and her slender tongue flicks out, like I wish it would over my cock.

I palm my cock and stroke it. Her chest pumps faster, her breathing audible.

If she likes to watch me make myself come, I will do it, but I despair of it relieving any of the burning in me. Each orgasm makes it worse. Like giving in to it only increases the depth of my thrall. And each time I see her come, it is like she is imprinting herself deeper and deeper into me.

Soon, she will be so etched into the essence of who I am I will not be able to get her out of me. Physically.

That this is the same female who only yesterday I believed a male—who yesterday had been encased in armor denying her femininity. She is now so feminine, so powerfully sensual, I am captivated.

When she comes, her body writhes—her hips thrusting against her hand, her back arching and legs widening. Her face contorts with the climax, but she doesn't take her eyes from me. She stares at my cock in my hand through her orgasm, as though watching me makes it better.

I am filled with jealousy—envious of her hand feeling her clench around her fingers. Envious of her other palm, caressing and squeezing her breasts.

Envious of the air filling her lungs. Envious of the leaves touching her legs, the rock supporting her back.

I would be all those things to her and more—if I could.

The hours pass, the heat of the day inexhaustible.

The two suns arch across the sky, seeming to descend. One disappears behind the horizon, but the other takes longer, stretching the twilight. The day is endless.

She fixes me with a come-fuck-me stare. She does not mean it. Or she does, but she does not really want me to do to her as her body is begging. She eases the ache of the burn by running her hands up and down her limbs. The sensation of touch making it easier to hold off orgasm again.

I do not bother touching myself. There is no easing it for

me.

Only distracting myself by watching her.

I let the longing to be fucking her lull me into a state of numbness.

I can feel her—how it would be to crawl to her and run my hands up her thighs. To spread her legs and sink my face into her wet folds. To taste her again… To feel her come on my tongue again… Hear her crying my name like it is a litany. Like I am her god and savior.

To rear over her and thrust into her.

My cock so deep inside her, my whole self disappears into her. I drive into her, my hips slapping against her thighs. I have to hold her down, to keep her from moving away from the force of my thrusts.

She clings to me, her fingers digging into my arms. "Oten! Yesss!" she cries, and it is a world-shattering sound.

One that triggers my senses.

One that makes me realize, I am not imagining this.

My eyes open, as if they were not before.

This is not happening merely in my mind. This is happening in actuality. I am actually fucking her with everything in me, and she is coming around me so hard, I have to grit my teeth to keep from following.

Her head falls back, and she screams to the sky.

Though her thighs hold me in her—I have to pull away.

She grabs for me and protests, "No!"

But I pull out, just in time, spilling my come across her belly. It jets onto her in rapid bursts, the silver liquid pooling then dripping across her. It streams into her navel and runs into the valley of her breasts, across the curves of her waist.

I hang my head from exhaustion.

I cannot believe… I do not understand…

I cannot remember…

"Why?" she thrashes her head, her eyes delirious. "Why

didn't you come in me?" She tries to sit up but can't, her body too wasted with the burning, with the sex. With everything.

I have to get it off her.

Her Ssedez-strengthened skin should protect her from my come seeping into her pores, but I cannot risk it.

She lies back on the ground, wasted with pleasure.

I want to join her, but I search for water, for cloth. I find some of each. I wash her. I clean her belly until it is as though my come never touched her.

Unclean—I feel as though I have committed some horrible sin that I do not understand.

Water. I must clean her.

I bathe her—wash her between her legs, her thighs, her breasts, to be sure I left nothing behind. I do not want to taint her. I worry my come will poison her somehow.

I refill the bottle from the stream, screw back on the top. It filters the water, and I take it back to her. I hold the bottle to her mouth, and she drinks without question.

She sleeps, and the sun goes down. My eyes are heavy, but I do not rest.

I watch her sleep and filter more water.

I urge her to drink.

The moons rise. There is a break in the trees, and the sky is bright despite the night, three moons lighting the sky. Though I cannot see through the trees. The moonlight leaves long shadows and broad patches of light.

My sense returns as the night air cools; the burning in my veins recedes. But the Attachment does not.

Her skin changes, the armor withdrawing. It smooths to its human texture. She's changing back.

The Ssedez in me mourns the change. But the part of me that has Attached to her is glad she is getting what she wants.

Her skin is no longer protected.

But I cannot force on her what she will not accept.

Chapter Fifteen

Nem

Water. It feels so good going down.

The pleasure of drinking pure H_2O is almost as good as his hands and arms lifting me to drink it. I do feel better. The burning in my blood lowers to a sizzle, and I remember.

I feel more human. More like myself. My tongue feels different; my skin feels different. Less like a Ssedez.

It's working.

And he's helping.

I remember—things that I forgot while consumed with the pain of needing to fuck—who I am, what I'm doing on this planet, who Oten is, and why I'm not supposed to fuck him.

He remembered. When I forgot.

I open my eyes and find him staring at me. His expression is unreadable in the darkness, but the tender touch of his hand on my cheek says more than his eyes ever could.

He cares.

I don't know why.

He has no reason to.

He has every reason to want me dead. He could've killed me multiple times by now.

Yet he's caring for me, righting his wrongs, small though they are in comparison to what humans have done to his kind.

I don't understand.

Even as I was begging for him to come in me, he pulled out.

That I could lose control of myself like that… It was from the burning but…it terrifies me. I shiver, thinking about it.

Thank every god there is, it eases when the suns go down.

The lethargy that the heat and the orgasms poured through my body subsides. Perhaps it's the changing, too, from human to Ssedez and back, that's contributing to my exhaustion. Going without sleep is usually easy for me — military training and all that.

Oten puts the water bottle to my lips again. I take it from his hand and sit up. I brush against his enormous body, enough to know he is still naked.

I shove that knowledge away.

I don't have to see him, so I don't need to think about him naked. Or what his ass feels like in my hands as he thrusts into me.

He backs away and says in that deep voice, "You are awake."

"No shit," I say but it comes out scratchy. I drink more, trying to dislodge the hoarseness in my throat. I clear my throat, and it gets no better.

I am hoarse from screaming while he fucked me.

Damn.

"Do you hurt?" he asks, and his concern irks me.

"Why do you care?" My voice is so low and throaty, like sex on a stick. Great.

"Because I do." His tone is as pointed as a laser.

I snort. "Just want to know when I'll be good to fuck again? Don't worry. I'm sure by the time the sun rises, I'll—"

"No!" He bellows so loud the night bugs stop chirping.

I shift away from him, trying to be unfazed by the force in his tone, trying not to be fascinated by his interest in me.

"I do not care when you will be 'good to fuck again.'" He uses a mocking tone and imitates my accent.

I roll my eyes, though he can't see them. "You will when the burning starts again. Tomorrow, I'll be just as mindless with the need to fuck as I was today. Don't worry." I try to make my words as bitter as possible. But it's too sharp. My anger is obvious. I drink more water.

"I do worry. But not for what you say."

"What do you worry then? That we'll find my crew, and they'll execute you on sight?" I should want that. I do. I absolutely do.

Not.

Fuck.

"I do not fear death, in any case."

I scoff in jealousy. I fear death more than anything. "Congratulations. You've conquered humanity's biggest phobia." I raise my water bottle in mock cheers to him.

"I have no need for your human jokes."

"Just a need for human pussy," I sneer.

I hear him breathing. Seething. He's mad. "I have no need for human *pussy*." He spits the word.

"You spent hours staring at mine!"

He growls, an edgy barbaric sound, then grasps my neck. "Listen." He brings my face to his, and I feel his breath on my cheeks. "I need *your* cunt. No one else's. I care not for humans. I just want yours."

It's almost frightening. The intensity of his words. As fierce as though he could be talking about killing me. Except he's talking about my cunt. Right. "Did you find utopia down there or something? Your tongue was so far up inside me, you had to be licking my cervix." I fail to conceal my curiosity. Is his tongue really that long, or did it just feel that way? Was it real, or an illusion like everything else this fucking planet makes me feel?

"Utopia?" he asks, confused. "This means a kind of paradise? Your taste has aphrodisiac qualities, if that's what you mean."

I'm not sure which is worse, knowing he likes the taste of me so much or that there's a note of longing in his tone, like he can't wait to taste me again. "Before you, yesterday, there were cobwebs down there so thick, I'm surprised it hadn't sealed shut."

"Cobwebs? This is a figure of speech, yes? There were no spiders in—"

I laugh. At least he's good for a joke.

He insists, "I care about much more than your readiness to fuck." The severity in his tone gives me chills, though now I've returned to human, I'm sweating.

He can't be as serious as he sounds.

"You mean the Ssedez?" I clarify. "You care about protecting your people." *Not about me.*

"I do." He strings along his tone as though he wants to say something but holds back. "And more." There's a softness to his words. It's enticing. It awakens my curiosity and quells my sarcasm.

I want to ask, *what else?* And no doubt he wants me to ask. But I can't think why. And for some reason, I can't shake the feeling I won't like the answer.

"Are you able to procreate?" he asks.

My mouth falls open. *What the—* "Excuse me?"

"Reproduction—is that something you are capable of?"

I cannot believe he asked that. The way he phrased it makes me feel like an incubator for having babies. "That's none of your business."

"It is possible, though I am not certain because my body is reacting strangely on this planet, but you could be carrying a child of mine right now."

The answer is a flat *no*, but I have no motivation to solve his problem when he's being a dick about it.

He softens his tone. "I have offended you. I do not mean to. I am unsure how to ask according to your customs."

"It's a little late for this conversation."

"What I mean is, it is obvious our genes are compatible given—"

"Given that you turned me into you!"

"Which I am trying to help rectify. Do you need more water?" He reaches for the bottle.

I pull it away. "I'll get it." I stand to get farther from him and go refill my bottle. His fake caring for me annoys me.

I go to the stream, following the sounds of the water, expecting to not be able to see it in the darkness.

But I can. The water, where it flows between the banks, is lit up in a rainbow array of colors—blues and pinks and yellows. Like someone filled it with strings of multicolored lights.

Except…they swim. Like fish.

I stand and watch it twinkle.

"It is beautiful," Oten says from behind me. "We had similar creatures on our home world. We called them—well, it translates to Lover's Light Fish."

"Lover's Light?" I can't stop staring at them enough to be annoyed at him for following me. In the darkened water, they blink like stars in the night sky.

"There is a story of a male Ssedez losing himself to the blinking lights—as he would to one he fell in love with at first sight. He fell into the water and was poisoned to death by them."

"Poison?"

"Do not let one touch your skin or get into your water bottle. If they are anything like the Lover's Light, one bite will give you great pain. Two bites will stop your heart."

"Figures something so beautiful would be deadly."

"Yes. It figures." He echoes my phrase with the awkwardness of someone who is learning my speech idioms.

I look at him a moment. My language is not his language. And yet he knows it fluently. Very well. He's studied it, in depth. I wonder why.

I kneel on the bank, filling the bottle carefully out of the way of the fish. They float leisurely, and none of them come toward me as I disturb the water. "They're not aggressive."

"They don't need to be. Their prey comes to them."

"Kind of like you," I say, intending it to be too low for him to hear. From the first time I saw his fangs, it was like being hypnotized into the need to be bitten. I don't know how much of it is this place versus just him.

But his hearing is better than I thought. "I had no intention of luring you in, if it means anything. It is this place. Normally, I can control my fangs."

"I suppose it's something." I stand and watch the filter laser light up the bottle, then, once it's done, I drink. My bladder is protesting, so I sneak into the woods to pee.

Leaves brush my leg, and I suck air through my teeth at the slice of pain. *Shit.* I touch the spot, and my fingers come away damp. I guess my protective armor really has retreated. My skin is back to its normal, vulnerable, human self.

I gingerly step between the plants, thanks to the moonlight lighting my path. I wish I could stop my pangs of regret—disappointment that I am vulnerable to the plant life once more. I did not want to be Ssedez, but it had its perks. Being able to move fast today was nice, too.

I wonder if it would've made me immortal. Like him.

The thought fills me with a kind of euphoric power I never thought about. To be immortal—what would that be like? To never die? To see the universe change and change over centuries, never fearing for the end of life, knowing it will always continue.

Yet, the Ssedez do die. Somehow. The Ten Systems killed them, *en masse*. I suppose even impervious beings will die from lack of oxygen if their starship is destroyed, and they likely burn in an explosion.

A silence drums in my ears—louder than all the jungle noises. The animals stop their chirping and clicking.

There's a rustling in the brush on the other side of the stream.

And then more than a rustling—a painfully loud crack that sounds like a gigantic animal bumped a tree and trampled the plants around it. Those trees are huge, a hundred years old or more. Something big enough to move one would have to be—

I am naked, defenseless. Whatever it is, it would likely kill me in one swipe.

I race back to Oten, jumping over the leaves, trying to keep from cutting myself as best I can.

I see his outline in the moonlight.

He shoves my blaster into my arms then pulls us both down into a crouch. "I think it's a *bureuh*."

I recognize the word from one of the mythical stories of the Ssedez. "Those exist?" I can't believe that story is true. It can't be. If it was, the animal would be knocking these trees over, pulling them from the ground by the roots with its jaws.

"A relative," he whispers. "Not as large."

A rumble comes from the creature. It's a minor growl from its chest, but the bass is so low it vibrates through my body.

Oten and I turn in unison, following the sound of the

creature. It splashes through the stream, crossing to our side. Its shadow is almost visible in the moonlight.

"Try not to kill it," he murmurs.

"What?"

"They were rare in my world. Such large beasts, it is hard for them to survive in any environment."

"Fuck their survival. If it tries to kill me, I kill it."

He inhales to speak again, but the sounds of the *bureuh* get closer.

Oten wordlessly touches the handle of one of his knives to my leg. I take his offering. While I'm better with a blaster than a knife, in close combat, my blaster is useless. He knows it. A knife is better than my bare hands.

The animal crosses a large patch of moonlight, and I have to suppress a gasp. The shadow is three times my height. A dozen horns crown its head and line its shoulders.

One head butt from it, and I'd be impaled to death.

I've fought worse, but I tighten my stance, planning an attack. Assuming its teeth are as ferocious as its horns, going high will not be an option. Crouching low or veering to its side would be a better attack. Though if its night vision is good, rushing it from the side may not be an option.

Its head turns toward us, catching our scent.

Oten touches his hand to my thigh, and his finger taps a leftward direction. Then he leaves, sneaking silently into the brush.

Splitting up is a good idea. It will have to go after one of us. The other can ambush it from behind.

If it attacks.

It heads toward our gear, sniffing out our campsite.

Those are our survival supplies. Without them, we'll be as dead as we would be if the creature eats us.

I set my blaster to low and aim at a tree opposite our direction, hoping to distract it. I shoot, and the red laser lights up the night and lands with an explosion of sparks in the tree.

But it doesn't work. The creature is more intelligent than I supposed. It only glances at the tree, then turns its nose in my direction, the source of the blast.

It paws the ground and gives a preattack growl.

I hold my breath. Maybe it's not aggressive.

Then it charges.

It's fast, faster than something that size should be. I leap to the side. The force of my legs propels me a dozen feet, but I land in a roll. The plants slice dozens of cuts across my back and chest. I grit my teeth against the pain and land on my feet.

The creature rears to a stop and lifts its nose in the air. It follows my scent and pivots in my direction. It grunts and stamps at the ground, the impacts heavy enough to shake the ground beneath it.

I see movement behind the animal, and then I spot Oten in the moonlight, moving stealthily between the trees.

The animal snorts and raises its head. I fear it's about to charge me, but before it can, Oten leaps from his hiding spot onto the creature's neck. He grabs its horn, hanging on as the creature shakes and tries to toss Oten off its back.

Oten lifts his arm high and slices down with his knife.

The *bureuh* roars in pain and whips its head from side to side. Oten struggles to hang on and nearly drops his knife. He keeps his place and lands another wound with his knife.

He's not striking killing blows though, not aiming for its arteries or brain.

Stupid. But noble.

It's difficult to see, but there's a space visible between the animal's enormous fore and back legs. They're as big around as a tree, but there's room enough for me to dive between them—if it doesn't step on me. Its belly, from what I can tell, looks rounded and vulnerable. I don't see any sharp spikes.

The animal may or may not be rare on this planet, but if I have to make a choice between its life and Oten's... I charge the animal and lunge beneath it, ignoring the plants that tear through my skin. I reach out with Oten's knife and slice a deep gouge into the beast's belly. I scramble out the other side at the same time it bellows in pain.

It lurches upward onto its hind legs—tossing Oten off its back. Its roar sounds so loud in my ears, they ring.

It lands on its front paws again, the ground shaking with the impact. Then gallops off into the forest, knocking trees to the ground in its path.

I look for Oten, in the direction he was thrown, but am unable to see him in the dark.

"Oten!" I call.

No answer.

I expect him to stand, to see his shadow, to hear him move. Nothing.

I charge over to where I think he landed and search through the vegetation, ignoring all the cuts the leaves make into my skin. "Oten!"

He's near immortal. Something so simple as being thrown couldn't have hurt him. Okay, maybe twenty feet is a long way, and that beast was pretty strong.

I shout his name again.

The moonlight lights up a tree that has a fresh gash in its trunk—about the size of Oten's head.

No.

I crouch and search the area in front of the tree where he would have landed, pushing aside the leaves with my knife.

His dark figure lies beside a rock, on his side.

I land on my knees beside him. I call his name again, and he is unresponsive. I feel for his pulse.

Except it's impossible to feel. Not through his thick armor. I have no idea how to give first aid to a Ssedez. *Goddamn it!*

He can't die.

I don't want him to die. Which should be a surprise thought, but I don't have time to think about how I'm supposed to want him dead.

I keep his head aligned and roll him to his back. I hold my cheek near his face and feel his breath move against my skin.

That is some relief. He's breathing, but it doesn't stop my heart from pounding.

He's unconscious.

He hit his head. I run my hands over his scalp, through his hair, searching for a wound, an indentation, anything, and wish like hell I had a light. I don't feel any wounds. Even the tree and the force of the *bureuh's* throw could not pierce his natural armor.

It doesn't mean his brain didn't bruise internally against his skull. He could have a concussion.

But I don't get to find out.

The cuts I've been ignoring—the ones from countless leaves that are scattered all over my body—I can't ignore them anymore.

The burn, the desire that's been torturing me since landing in that escape pod—it's back. It's in my blood, my veins, and flowing toward my heart. Into my brain. I shake my limbs trying to get it to stop. To get it out of me. To stop it flowing.

My head grows light, my pulse erratic.

I'm going to pass out.

I scramble for my water, spots coloring my vision. I can't stand. I crawl across the ground. But more plants slice into me. And it's too much.

I collapse, unable to stand it.

I cry out from the pain, the flames raging through my body, like a fire scorching my heart.

Then everything goes dark.

Chapter Sixteen

Oten

The traces of sunlight penetrate my eyes and wake me.

My head feels like it's been pounded with an anvil, but otherwise I am fine.

Nem.

I jerk to sitting, scanning for her, but I don't see her. "Nem!" I cry.

She moans, somewhere ahead of me.

I go to her.

She lies in the grass, her skin as pale as the day I met her. And covered in red gashes all over her body—cuts from the plants.

Her eyes are barely open, but she sees me, reaches for me.

Her voice is a whisper, but she manages. "Help…" Sweat shines on her forehead and drips between her breasts. Her legs shake, and her nipples are so hard, they look like they might break if I touch them.

She lets out a cry so full of pain it reaches inside me and begs me to do something.

"You're burning? From the plants?" I want to help, but I have to know what kind of help she wants. If she wants an orgasm, I will give it to her. But there's more I can offer her.

"Yes." Her tongue does not linger over the "s," and I catch a glimpse of the tip, rounded and thick—human. She has turned back completely. Which is why she is so affected by her wounds.

I need to address them. They have scabbed over. She's not bleeding, but some look like they may fester without disinfectant. And I have something that can help more than any chemical she may have in the survival supplies.

I grasp her hand and raise it to my mouth, giving her ample time to refuse. My fangs are retracted, thankfully, my head pounding with too much pain to think of biting anyone. Even her.

I lick the nasty gash on the back of her hand. I slide my tongue over it from bottom to top. I press it closed, sealing the two sides of the cut back together, licking away the scab, too.

I pull back and look at my work. There is but a thin line left, which will heal before the day is over.

"Okay?" I hold her healed hand in front of her, so she sees what I've done.

Her eyes widen in surprise, and she whispers, "Good."

"There is no venom in my mouth right now. It will not infect you." She almost nods, but I need a full answer. "Will you let me close your wounds?"

She breathes, "Yes."

I go as quickly as I can as thoroughly as I can, one cut at a time.

I start at her chest and work my way down her front. Luckily, the center of her breasts was spared; she must have subconsciously protected them. But her legs, from her thighs down, are worst.

I count thirty at least.

Her breathing is heavy and audible, her eyes closed. I lift up to turn her over, knowing there must be more on her back.

But she reaches for my head and pushes it down to the apex of her thighs. "Please," she begs.

I salivate with relief and have to stop myself from thanking her. She cannot know that every inch of her I taste makes me want to lick between her legs more.

She helps me spread her thighs wide. I close a few cuts on the way I had missed, then lower my head between her legs.

Her cunt is as lush and pink as I remember. I stroke her with my thumb, just glorying in the sight of her. I will not rush this, or hurry mindlessly like yesterday.

I lift the hood over her clit with my thumb and stroke her beneath it.

"Oten," she moans and lifts her hips closer to my touch.

I stare at her face a moment. Her head thrashing side to side, her eyes closed.

She can barely utter a sentence, but she calls out my name.

That more than even the sight of her ready and waiting sends a bolt of arousal to my cock. It hardens and thickens with the desire to be in her.

But I ready my tongue instead.

I hold her open with my hands and lick inside her. She tastes like female and sex, like the hottest sun and the sweetest honey, like power and strength. I feel it seeping into me as I lick between her wet folds, exploring and searching her.

I dip my tongue inside her, circling her opening then stroking in as deep as I can go. I find the round bulb inside and flick my tongue across it.

She writhes and presses harder against my face. The

wetness of her covers my cheeks, my nose—the scent filling my lungs.

I give her more, brushing my tongue around the spot inside her that she likes. Back and forth, circling and sliding. I press the tip of my nose to her clit, and it rubs back and forth in time with my tongue.

Her cries are music, and she calls out my name. I give her everything she asks; the need to satisfy her—that she wants me to satisfy her—spurs me to make it as good for her as I can.

She inhales hard and starts to tighten.

I have given her a dozen orgasms in the last two days. I know she's about to come.

So I slow down; I tune my tongue to the gasps in her breathing, drawing out her climax for as long as I can. She keens in her throat, her back arches, her body strains.

Then let's go.

She spasms around my tongue in tight clenches. I dip my fingers in, giving her something to squeeze and more relief. Her hips roll out the orgasm, and she goes limp. Her knees fall wide, and she lies replete on the ground.

She opens her eyes, and her stare is full of gratitude. "Thank you."

I shift my hardened cock with my hand, attempting and failing to ease it. "It is my pleasure."

She gives a half smile. "If you say so."

I stroke her cheek, tracing the splashes of red blooming in her complexion. "I do say." There is no small amount of surprise at myself and how much I mean that. I want to give her everything. To satisfy her every need, to heal her and protect her and take care of her.

I am losing the fight against myself.

She is courageous and has done nothing but work with me since we were marooned here yesterday. The teamwork we used to get rid of the beast last night was seamless. I'm forced to admit, we work well together.

My ability to hate her is waning beneath the strength of my body's unwavering Attachment to her.

She searches my face with confusion but doesn't say anything. She does not pull away or grab my hand from her face. Her lips part like she means to ask a question but changes her mind.

"You have more cuts on your back," I say.

She squirms in discomfort and makes to roll over. "Yeah."

"Wait." I grab the pack and spread out the ground cloth. "Lie on this." I'd rather her not be entirely covered in dirt.

She does as I say and rests on her stomach on the tarp without complaint.

Her back is a mess of cuts and dirt. I have to clean it before I can heal anything.

I filter water and clean a rag from the survival supplies. It takes multiple rinsings of the rag and refills to the water bottle, but I get her clean. She's asleep by the time I'm done, and I start closing the myriad cuts with my tongue.

I have to find some way to keep her skin protected from the undergrowth while we travel to her fallen ship. Her white skin suit, which never helped at all, is in a heap of rags on the ground.

There is extra clothing in the survival pack, but it's thick and insulated. Meant for an emergency on an arctic planet. Even if I cut out the insulation, the material won't breathe.

My leather pants are more breathable, and they are resistant to the leaves. They are covered in scratches but have no holes.

I take off my pants and clean them, wiping them down on the inside and outside, then fashion myself a breech cloth out of her torn skin suit. I use string from the survival pack to make a belt for myself.

I've managed to only bring myself to orgasm twice in the hours of the morning. I had to relieve the pressure. Without it, my mind fogs, and my reason fades.

It gives me an idea. The last two days, we have tried to avoid having sex and ended up losing our sanity, only to have massive amounts of sex anyway. I wonder if every few hours we stopped to satisfy the burn and gave into having sex, maybe we could avoid going insane by the end of the day.

Nem wakes, her eyes opening as she sits in one motion. She glances at the sky, sees the twin sun almost overhead, and shakes her head. "We have to move."

"I agree."

She glances over at me finally and gapes. "Why aren't you wearing pants?"

"These are for you." I hand her my leather ones.

She looks at them skeptically. "Why?"

"We do not want this happening again. If I had a shirt, I would give it to you, too."

"Why do you care?" She does not cower from me, she's not afraid, but she looks at the leather as though it may bite her if she touches it. "Why are you helping me?"

"Because I am."

"There's a reason. What is it?"

"It is not what you thought before. It is not about the sex."

"I noticed. You could've fucked me multiple times in the last few hours because I would have let you."

I am burning already. The flames licking through my veins. The desire to touch her, to sink my cock into her, is there. But what is more present is this protective urge that I cannot ignore.

I have to give her an answer. Explaining the Attachment, which I hardly want to admit to myself is happening, is not an option. "I am not a barbarian. I would not force myself on someone when they are unconscious."

She grasps the leather and inspects it. "And these?"

"I do not want you to hurt either. Not when I can help."

"You could've just bitten me again."

I stiffen. There is no disdain in her tone. "Is that what you want?"

She meets my eyes, and her expression is unreadable. She is masking her emotions, hiding something from me.

I almost reach for her hand. I cannot help leaning toward her. She glances at my mouth. To kiss her, to meet her mouth with mine…I want it. To stroke her jaw, to feel her tender human skin and its precious softness.

Her eyes linger over my mouth, too, and her tongue licks her lower lip.

"I don't want you to bite me," she whispers.

"I will not." I have a newfound self-control when it comes to her. My fangs are retracted, and they will not come down—no matter how badly it hurts.

She leans forward and kisses me.

Chapter Seventeen

Nem

I have no idea why I'm kissing him. All I know is I want to.

His lips are smooth and unhurried. I feel the tension in him. I see it in his hardened cock, but he sheathes it. It's just a kiss; it's not a desperation for sex.

I don't think.

I'm trying to understand. He has every reason to hate me, to kill me, or at least take advantage of me. Humans butchered his kind in an aggressive war. He attacked my ship. He's supposed to want me dead.

Except he's taking care of me. And I don't understand why.

But I like it.

The way he kissed my wounds closed, the way he made me come with his mouth, it was almost like he cared for me. I can't explain it. But his kisses feel like more of the same.

He strokes my tongue with his like he's savoring me. Like he doesn't want to take from me. Like he only wants to accept what I give him.

I grab him to me and rise on my knees. I sink my fingers in soft, gold hair, and press him closer. His arms come around me.

His tongue reaches into my mouth and wraps around mine and tugs. I crush my mouth hard against his, begging him deeper.

He gives me what I want and presses his bare chest to mine, sealing us together.

I never thought I could want a kiss to go on forever. But I do.

I want him, Oten, to want me the way he is kissing me now—to care about me as he is caring for me—to value my humanity, as he is doing by healing me and helping me protect my skin.

I like it, too much. This being cared for. Being valued. Not having to worry about anyone else. Not having to be in charge of my crew. The responsibility of being a general, of having so many lives depending on me, is a heavy burden.

With his mouth on mine like this, it's as though I'm important for being me.

Him kissing me has everything to do with me. He has no reason to touch me like this except because he wants to. Pleasure in anything, especially myself, is not something I've ever had time for. But with him—Oten—I want to spend all the time there is doing nothing except touching him and making us feel good.

He caresses my cheek again, and he's so gentle, it's like being stroked with a feather. "I have a proposition."

I stare at his eyes, dark and depthless. The irises are black, but his gaze is not.

I don't let go of him. "What?"

"A schedule. A way to stay ahead of the burning madness."

I relax backward. "I'm listening."

He runs his hands down my arms, as if treasuring the feel of my skin. "Every day at its hottest, we lose our sanity to the need for sex. But what if we stay ahead of the need?"

"You mean give in to it before it incapacitates us?"

He nods. "Every few hours, we plan to stop and satisfy it. Then start moving again."

"So that when it's at its worst, we won't already be weakened. We'll be at our strongest."

A broad smile stretches my cheeks, but I have no desire to conceal it. "I love that idea." Not only because it makes strategic sense, but because more sex with him…yes, please. I want his touch like an engine craves fuel. It goes beyond the crazed desire this place makes me feel.

This planet doesn't have the power to make me want him and him alone.

His lips part, and he looks ready to say a thousand things, things that will still not just my desire, but my heart. Mine thuds so loud behind my ribs, I'm sure he can hear it beating.

He swallows and merely says, "We make a good team." He scratches his head. "I never thought I could say that about a human."

"Not all humans are the same. Not all of us want to dominate and destroy."

He stares at me quietly, as though remeasuring me. "You have honor."

"Is that a bit of respect I'm hearing?"

He nods, carefully, unable to take his eyes off me.

I don't know what is happening between me and this male who should hate me—who I should hate, too. It's as though because our bodies have proven such a perfect match, the rest of us—our feelings—can't help but follow.

It's as terrifying as any enemy I've ever faced. Far scarier than the *bureuh* charging me last night. I'm better off alone, separate, away from everyone and everything. I keep my distance; that's my MO.

Feeling for anyone—friend, lover, family—is not something I've allowed myself since my parents died. I've had too many things to do for my own survival, for the survival of the mission. That I could be feeling something for him, the male who ordered an attack on my ship and killed members of my crew...

It makes no sense. It can't happen.

As though he can see the fear written on my face, his expression changes. Heat—he lets it pump through his eyes, and he drops his gaze to my body.

"You want it, don't you?" He traces his finger delicate as a flower petal around the underside of my breast. "You want my cock inside you, filling you."

"Yes." I close my eyes.

"You want me pounding it into you until you're screaming."

I shiver, and my lips part.

"But how do you want it?"

"Hard," I groan, growing wet between my legs. I can feel him. Remember him doing it to me.

He runs his hand down my leg and grips my thigh. "Fast or slow?"

"Both." His fingers sinking into my soft flesh make me want him to stroke my swelling clit, too.

He lowers his mouth to my ear. "But I will lick your sweet cunt first. Would you like that?"

I shudder and lean against him. "Yes."

"And after you have come so many times you're begging me to stop, I will come on you."

I can see it again. His bright silver come pouring onto my belly.

"Not your belly," he corrects as though he can hear my

thoughts. "Your back."

There it is—the whole scene. Him forcing me to all fours and fucking me from behind. My mouth is open, and I'm panting. My inner thighs are wet, and I'm throbbing between my legs. I want it now.

"Later." He smacks my ass with a hard crack that makes me whimper and cling to him. "Get dressed." He picks up his pants and hands them to me.

My legs wobbling, I grab his leather pants and draw them up my legs.

He packs up the ground covering and stuffs it in the pack. He hands me a ration bar from the pack, and I eat. But he starts eating what looks like a yellow piece of fresh fruit.

"What's that?" I ask, my voice still throaty like sex—which I'm still desperate for.

He pulls the fruit back from his mouth, and I see his fangs extended.

I back away from him. "Put those things away."

"I'm staying ahead of the need, relieving some of the venom this way." He sinks them into the fruit again and takes a bite.

"Is it working?"

He chews and says around the food. "I haven't bitten you since I started eating these yesterday."

"They don't have more of the compound that's causing the burning?"

"Perhaps. But it is better than biting you."

I nod and roll up the cuffs of his pants so they're still covering my boots.

I'm covered from the waist down. From the waist up, however, I'm topless. It's not terrible. I don't have breasts enough to bounce much, and my chest muscles are firm from my decades of training.

I strap on my weapons belt, my blaster holstered. His

machete in my one hand, my computer in the other, I am ready to make tracks.

Oten stands staring at me.

I can't help staring back. He is naked but for his chest holster, the pack on his back, and a white cloth he's strapped over his groin.

His legs—his thighs bulge with muscle. His lower abs make a V trailing down between his hips. I guess that male attribute is not so uniquely human.

His arms and his chest—*damn*—I'd noticed but hadn't allowed myself to really look. He is a fantasy come to life. Enormous, virile, overpowering, and he's looking at me like I am the same.

He points in the direction we need to go. "Let us move now before—"

"Before we can't. Yeah." I tear my eyes from him and lead the way.

I don't have to hack a trail for the first half mile, so we're able to run. We follow the destructive path of the *bureuh* from last night.

"You really have these creatures on your home world?" I ask, nodding to the gouges in the soil from the beast's claws and the felled trees from the beast's horns.

"These among others."

I keep a steady pace so my breathing stays even as I speak. "Did you use them in battle?"

He laughs, low in the barrel of his chest. "We are peace-loving, the Ssedez. We train for battle defense only. The only wars we have fought in our written history have been against the Ten Systems."

"But you have a history of being great warriors."

"For sport. Not for war among our own kind."

It's exciting to learn. The idea a species could evolve without civil war—something humans could never claim.

"Humans have warred among themselves since the dawn of our time."

"I know." The anger in his tone has bite, as though his fangs are out.

"Not all of us are warmongers though."

"Not that you know anyone like that."

I glance at my computer and course correct off the path of the *bureuh*. Our pace is forced to slow as I carve through the plants with the knife. "I know many humans who would prefer to never war ever again." Myself included.

"You are a conquering species. That is what you do. Take control of other species and their worlds for your gain."

"Some of us want to change that."

"You cannot change the very nature of a species. It is in your genes."

I stop and face him. "When was the last time you met a human?"

He stops, too, the rage our conversation has awakened in him tense over his face. "Before you, not since our last battle a hundred years ago."

I quip with sarcasm, "You had lots of lengthy conversations with each of these individuals on their personal opinions about the war they were forced to fight?"

"Forced to fight? They volunteered."

"No." I shake my head. "You know nothing about the Ten Systems and their recruitment practices. Not a single one is a volunteer. Every human is genetically tested, and if we pass their tests, we're forced to enlist."

"*You* were forced?"

"I wanted to join. For personal reasons. That I would inherit the DNA from my parents who were both in the military was a given."

He pauses and seems to contemplate this. "I was a newly trained warrior when the war began. We fought off your offensives for fifty years, and never once did you engage diplomacy."

"Not me. Them. I was not alive then. My parents weren't alive either."

"Doesn't matter. You're all the same."

"How do you know?" I cross my arms, losing patience with his judgmental obstinacy.

He bends his face to mine. "Some things do not change. No pretend mask or lies will convince me otherwise."

I want to kick him. Hit him. Punch him. "How can you care for me when I'm unconscious, heal my wounds with your own mouth, go naked so you can clothe me, and still hate my species so much?"

His nostrils flare, and his hands twitch like he's nervous. "I do not know."

"You're lying. You know why."

He growls, aggressive, a warning.

I ready my knife hand, on instinct, but I know he won't attack me. "Tell me."

"It is a side effect."

I wait for him to explain, but he doesn't. "Of what?"

"Of having intercourse with you. You became no longer just any human I could kill."

It's my turn to growl. "Like once mated, you own me or something? I don't think so."

He looks away from me. "It is much more complicated than that." But rather than tell me, he grabs the machete from my hand and walks around me.

He slices a path for us with such ferocity, I fear he'll kill animals as well as plants.

I'm not going to argue with him. He works faster than me. Which I will not complain about. The faster we move, the faster we get to my crew.

The conversation stalls after that, the burn of the

atmosphere getting to us.

I'm able to calculate our rate of travel and the approximate distance to my ship's crash-landing site. If we keep this pace, we should reach it tomorrow.

There's an elevation gain coming—like there's a mountain in our way. I have no idea how to account for that. We'll figure it out when we get there.

The desire rages through me—the ache throbbing in my clit like an insatiable demand. I feel empty to my core. Moving is painful, each step rubbing me in places that don't want to be rubbed. Or they do, just not from walking.

I touch myself subconsciously, seeking to ease the discomfort. But it makes it worse. I pull my hand away, only to touch myself again minutes later.

Watching him walk in front of me, his shoulders and arms tensing with each swing of the knife, his stride long and fluid, every muscle in his body working—I grow weak with wanting him.

He munches on the fruit he plucks from bushes at a more rapid rate.

It must be filling him with the desire toxin, but he eats more, not less. His progress slows, and I see his free hand, between pieces of fruit, adjusting his cock more than once.

It's time for our scheduled break.

But my mouth is so slack from drooling over him, I can't get the words out to tell him.

I tell him by touch instead, grabbing his bicep, unable to not squeeze the hard muscle and feel it.

He stops, his breathing ragged.

I unbuckle my weapons and drop them to the ground. I take the pack from his shoulders then press my bare breasts to his arm.

He groans but doesn't face me. I run my hand over his torso, tracing his knife harnesses, then feeling the washboard of his abs and downward. Down, down, down until I cup his rigid cock.

I drop my forehead to his shoulder and stroke him through the fabric he has tied around his waist. Wetness pools between my legs, dampening his leather pants I'm wearing. I'm already envisioning his cock in me, easing the ache inside me, stretching me. He's so big, it's impossible for me to take more of him.

He turns his head to me, the tips of his fangs retracting into his upper jaw.

I don't want to know the amount of self-control it takes him to do that.

"Break time?" he asks in a deep grumble. His gaze is heavy over me, sweeping over my mouth and my neck. He caresses the side of my breast, and I pull back so he can circle my nipple with his fingers.

"Yes," I breathe, tipping my head up toward his mouth.

He takes my face in his hands and crushes his mouth to mine.

There is no savoring or hesitation. Just lust. From his lips. From his tongue. They seize mine, take over me, and I am on the ground.

He tears his weapons from his chest, then weighs me down. His hard cock is already rubbing me where I want him, my legs already wrapping around his hips.

The urgency—the natural lust already between us, combined with the madness of this place—has us bursting with the need to fuck. Like two combustible machines racing toward each other. We'll detonate whether we collide or not. But how much more explosive the fire will be if we incinerate together.

I wriggle off his leather pants, rolling over and kicking one leg out.

He frees his cock.

I am pulled to my knees. I spread my thighs wide, my ass in the air, and he thrusts into me from behind.

His cock—his wide, long, enormous cock—stretches me to my limit and burrows deep within me. Then he grows impossibly bigger, excruciatingly harder, until I am so full, stoked in so many intimate places. So primed and aroused, so wet and swollen. My mind and body so overtaken, I am carnal. There is no way for me to respond except by instinct.

The brutal, consuming need to fuck.

He drives into me once, twice, three times and—

I scream and call for him. "Oten!" The orgasm storms through me, tearing up my spine, searing my nerves with fierce and unending pleasure.

He pounds me again and again. Slapping against me, pulling me to him.

Where my mind ends and his body begins, the boundary blurs until I am only sex.

Sex and ecstasy.

They are me.

And he is mine.

I dig my fingers into the dirt. Grip the ground with all the strength in my hands and shove myself back into his thrusts, every muscle in my body forced to its limit.

I meet his drives. Making it harder, faster, until my flesh is shaking and my skin vibrating. My bones, my whole being shudders and is swept away on the bliss of coming around his cock.

I imagine what it would be like to watch us—for someone to come upon us in the jungle. To be seen in this way, to be witnessed as a purely sexual creature—

But, on the pain of my existence, as though I'm robbed of the very thing I was made to have, he pulls of out me without coming.

I turn to him and snarl, almost animal-like.

But I get to watch. He grips his cock, his face a torn portrait of agony. He roars a great sound, and with killing tension seizing his limbs, he comes. His sparkling liquid silver seed spills in the dirt.

I am horrified.

It's a stunning waste of beauty.

I wanted that.

I needed that.

Why did he deny me? How could he make me crave him like that and then take it away from me?

He raises his eyes to me, his breathing like a storm blowing in and out of his lungs. "I...couldn't—" He forces himself to swallow. "I...almost...didn't...stop."

Then I remember.

He's doing what I asked him to. To keep from turning me.

He collapses on his back next to me, and I stare at him. He really has godlike powers. His ability to resist the insanity of this place is inhuman. Which makes sense because he's not human.

I lay back, recovering, my body overwrought and hammered.

I don't know how I'm going to survive this for another day without losing my mind to him.

Chapter Eighteen

OTEN

She will be the death of me. This thing between us, just when I think it cannot get worse, it does.

We do it again: hike for a few hours, then stop when the burning becomes too much.

I fear hurting her, but not enough to be able to refuse her. I make her come with my mouth this time. She uses her tongue then her hand on me.

She makes me come on her back like I promised. The look of longing on her face as my come spouts from my cock should make me happy. She wants me to come in her—in her greedy cunt or her succulent mouth.

But I cannot.

It makes me wish I were human so that I could.

That I think this is horrific. Wishing I were human is a monstrous betrayal of everything I believe. I stay away from her for a while after that. Letting her lead, following far behind.

She does not seem to mind.

I think she is as shocked as I am by how much she wants me to come in her.

It makes no sense. But the part of me that is forming the physical Attachment to her is pleased. Each time I fuck her, each time I make her come, she becomes more attached to me, too, giving me a deep satisfaction.

It is true that I still hate her kind.

But my regard for her, my respect, is growing. I think—I am still in doubt—but I may be starting to trust her. Which is dangerous and foolish, but I cannot help relying on her steadfast abilities, how trusting and freely she lends both them and her insatiable body.

This place makes her want sex, yes, but I believe it does not force her to desire *me* as she does.

It pleases me. Too much.

And I fear, am horrified at the possibility, that my feelings could potentially Attach to her like I have physically. It is unthinkable.

Being with her is impossible in any case.

I do not know what will happen once we reach her ship, if we find her crew. They will likely imprison me.

I wonder if she will let that happen.

The heat of the day rises. We fuck again, and though I intend to be gentle, she makes it impossible. She demands, and I succumb. I have no choice but to give to her what she cries out for.

To see her satisfied is the fulfillment of my existence.

Denying her the pleasure of my coming inside her is the hardest thing I have ever had to do.

My body is made for such marathon sex. We Ssedez are built to withstand the demands of the Attachment mating period. But I am not made to restrain myself, too.

It drains me, and I become less focused on our path. I

blindly follow wherever she leads.

I worry about her body. Her sensitive human flesh.

So much sex cannot be good for her.

But it pleases me that she not only takes it but wants more at the same rate as I do.

I choose not to care whether it is because of me or because of the toxicity of this place. I care only that she wants me to fuck her. That is enough.

At least for now. When we reach her crew, I do not know what will happen to me or her. Or us.

The trail comes to the base of a cliff, an upward climb of rigid stone.

"Must we ascend?" I ask, but I do not look at her. I do not want her to see my fangs. They are extended, and my self-control needed to sheathe them is weakening.

We look up the cliff face, a wall of cragged gray rock so high, we're unable to see the top. Low-hanging clouds block the view.

"How are your climbing skills?" she asks.

"Not as good as my fighting skills." I wander along the cliff face. "We could try to find a way around."

"According to my topographical reading"—she stares at her computer—"this cliff extends far to the north. The *Origin* landed to the west. It would take us three days to go around."

She grips the rock with her hands, testing it. "The rock is solid." She takes out a knife, leans her ear into the stone and taps it with the metal hilt. "It's sound."

She stows the knife in her belt and climbs onto the wall. Her limbs are lithe and swift, her testing of the handholds and footholds quick and practiced.

I am outclassed, already, and she has only gone ten feet.

My muscle-heavy torso does not climb well. Plus, the survival pack will overthrow my balance. "I cannot climb and carry this load. We will have to leave it."

She hangs by one arm and stares down at me. "Seriously?"

I stare back and imitate her, "Seriously."

She laughs and pushes off the wall. She lands in a crouch. "We'll need to unload it." She dumps the pack and leaves behind the cold weather gear, the stove, and the extreme first-aid supplies. She keeps the bare minimum, then binds the pack with twine, making it as thin as possible. "I'll need it close to my back."

I gaze up the wall, concerned for us both. "I wish we had a rope."

"Without a belay device or pitons, it's useless."

I do not know what those are, but I do not ask. It makes no difference. She anchors the pack to her back and begins her climb. I watch her.

Following her path will do me no good. My body is too big to use the same hand and footholds as her.

"Don't climb beneath me," she calls down. "In case any rock breaks loose."

I do as she says and start to climb to her left. I am slow and clumsy at first, but I find a rhythm. I get stuck sometimes and have to downclimb and go up a different way.

It is unbelievable how much faster Nem moves than me. She becomes a speck above me.

I reach a spot in the rock that changes to a darker graphite gray. I climb around it and farther up see water dripping down the face.

Visibility grows poor, and I realize, I have climbed into the cloud.

And lost sight of Nem completely.

I swear in my own language but keep climbing. I will find her at the top.

But my mind grows delirious.

I'm breathing in the vapor of the cloud—and it is full of the desire toxin.

My lungs burn as though enflamed. I start hallucinating.

More than once I stop, thinking it's her tight breasts and hardened nipples in my hands. Then I remember, it's just rock.

I keep climbing. The rock grows wetter, and sprouts of moss dot the best handholds. My options for purchase grow more difficult. My mind slips away until I can no longer remember why I'm climbing or where I'm going to—only that I have to get to her.

I need her like I need breath. I need to know she is okay. I call her name, "Nem!" but get no response.

My body pulses with the need for her, but more strongly is my mind's panic over the need to protect her. I climb onward—focused yet brainless.

I hear her voice on the air. A cry. I know that sound.

She needs me.

"Nem!" I climb farther, not knowing which direction her call came from.

"Oten!" she shouts in pain.

The sound comes to my right. I climb sideways, the cloud thickening until I can barely see my own hands.

Her voice calls again and again. And I follow it, despairing that I'll find her.

"I'm coming!" I call back to her as her voice grows nearer.

"Hurry!" By her tone, the cry, I know the sound. She is not injured. Though she is in pain, it is from the burn, the air in our lungs, the desire leaching through her body. It steals all will for anything other than sex.

Her cries are closer and turn to moans. Each one shoots into me, arousing my cock until it's throbbing like needles will pierce it if it's not relieved.

My hand reaches out and hits air, not rock. I curve around a corner in the rock and find a ledge with my knee.

"Oten…" she calls, breathless, and the cloud parts so I

see her.

The ledge is a cave, a cavern in the wall, and she lies in the back on a bed of green moss. Naked, shivering, she has her fingers between her legs, kneading and working.

At the sight of me, her face twists, and her back arches—all the signs I recognize, she's coming.

"Help me..." she cries then her face contorts in an agonizing climax.

I tear off the cloth restraining my groin, toss my weapons on her pile of things, and crawl between her legs. I grab her hands away, and she moans, tears pouring from her eyes.

"Please..." she seethes through her teeth.

Her cunt is soaking. My cock is hard as steel.

I thrust into her, and the pleasure is tormenting.

She grips my cock in a tight fist. I have to drive into her again, hard, with the full force of my body.

"Yes!" she screams and is never silent after that. She moans on my every retraction and cries each time I dive back in. Over and over, until I fear her voice will be gone before I am done.

Her gaze is delirious. Her eyes clouded. Her head thrashing side to side.

I start to come, unable to stop the growing power in me.

But I cling to the fine hairs of my control.

I must pull out. I must.

She yanks my head down to hers and growls, "Come in me."

I grit out, "Can't." I stop my hips, grinding my teeth against the violent need to pour into her.

She thrusts her hips against me, teasing me, taunting me. "I don't care. Come in me. Make me yours." Her words are so clear, she sounds almost lucid.

It calls to me. It appeals to my baser nature, my visceral need to claim her. For her to want me to claim her.

But her eyes tell the truth. She's not herself. The lust is driving her words. She's not deciding in her right mind.

She sees me trying to pull away and digs her nails into my ass and milks me with her cunt. I feel her squeezing my cock in intentional spasms. She will do anything to make me come in her.

But I can't.

I tear her hands away and spill it on the mossy ground. I cry out in agony, expecting it to bring relief. It doesn't. My lungs are pumping fire into my blood, blazing through my veins.

My cock does not soften, and the torture is brutal.

Her aggression does not abate. She grabs my shoulders and slams me to my back. She's on me, her mouth swallowing my cock.

I lose my rationale. All I can think or feel is what she's doing to me. The blissful plateau I ride while she sucks on my cock like it is her meal and sustenance.

She straddles me and rides me.

It hurts. But I cannot stop. I do not want her to stop. My brain feels like it's melting. The ability to decipher sensations burns away in the flames that only grow hotter.

I am on fire. And she burns with me.

I pull her off me before I come. I do not know why anymore. I just do it by rote, my seed pumping from my cock, the silvery liquid pooling on the green moss.

It does not end.

She's crying in pain. I know we should stop, but she reaches for me again.

I lose all sense of space and time, awareness of feeling.

I am only flames. And she my air.

As long as she is beside me, I will burn and endure the pain.

If she were not here, I would jump from the cliff to make

the torture end—the pain so terrible, I fear death may be the only escape from it.

Tears pour down her face. It hurts her. I'm hurting her. But still she cries for more.

I stop trying to fuck her. I use my hand and my tongue.

She tries to climb on me again, but her body is tense in agony, and I hold her off me.

My cock chafes. I do not want to touch it. I do not want it to feel anything else. But I cannot stop. She uses her mouth on me. It is the only relief there is. But continually fighting her, keeping her from swallowing as I come, exhausts me.

She is an insatiable sexual creature.

That is what we are, creatures. Animals.

The world goes dark, but the cloud still surrounds us, and the burning does not end.

I lie on my back, each breath I pull into my lungs cuts like a new incision in my chest.

She wheezes beside me.

We drift out of consciousness. I fear we are suffocating. We will die.

I do not know how to save us.

Chapter Nineteen

Nem

I am pain.

And Oten is my partner in the torture.

I loathe my need to be touched. It's not my own. But if I have to be touched I want it to be him.

He's gentler with me than I am with myself and gives me as much satisfaction as he can without hurting me.

But he denies me, too.

I spasm through orgasms, needing him to come in me. Like I am dying of thirst for him. My throat convulses each time he pulls out of my mouth.

I know why he does it. Or I used to know why he keeps emptying his come on the ground instead of inside me. I know I should want this. But it hurts. The dreadful pain of not being satisfied eats me.

I drift from consciousness, resurfacing when the pain gets too bad. I call to him, and he helps me. He calls to me, and I help him.

We are partners.

My lungs contract with the burning sensation, and my breathing becomes ragged. I get weak, so weak that to breathe becomes a labor.

Then everything goes dark.

Voices.

Movement.

A smooth liquid down my throat.

More darkness.

The world comes back after I don't know how long. I notice first that he's not near me. I don't even have my eyes open and I know. I had no idea I'd learned to know him just by feeling his presence. Until he's gone.

Sound returns to my ears.

Women's voices. Ones I don't recognize, except that they're human. I lie on something soft—a bed. The air I breathe is clear. I'm covered in a light sheet.

My eyes flutter open.

The cave is gone. I stare at a shiny metallic ceiling.

"Hello there," a voice says. A woman sits beside me—dark hair, kind eyes, concern wrinkling her brows. "Can you drink?"

A gentle arm lifts my head, and a cup is pressed to my lips.

The water sliding down my throat is a life-giving elixir.

"Not so fast," the woman says, and lowers the cup from my lips. "A little bit at a time." She brushes my face with her hand, and the gesture is so comforting, I turn my cheek into her palm and rest it there.

"It's all right," she soothes. "You'll have your strength back soon." She holds my hand with her other hand. I can't remember the last time I took comfort in the touch of another woman. It's like a balm after the striving and the fighting—and the pain.

Something about the woman, her voice, her energy seems familiar, and taking comfort from her seems so easy and natural. But I don't have the faculties to question it.

"What's your name, dear?" she asks.

Something amazing happens. A name, my true name, that I haven't thought in years—*Nemona*. I haven't gone by that name since I was a child. Since before I entered military school at fifteen.

"Nem—" My voice catches, and I have to cough. I try to sit up, but a horrible pain low in my body pushes me to lie back down. I roll to the side, hacking hard, like a bag of needles lodged in my throat and won't come out.

I expect the woman to pat my back or say something else comforting, but she doesn't.

My cough finally subsides, and I look up at her.

All her kindness is gone, and she is stiff beside me. "Nem? As in General Nem?"

I clear my throat again and nod, afraid to speak again.

She stands and puts space between us, letting me see her uniform. She's one of mine. An *Origin* crew member. A doctor by the rank insignia on her lapel.

"Leinit?" I choke out. That's why she's so familiar. She's my crew's chief medical officer.

"It's Leinita," she says with bitter disdain.

I lift my head. "You're alive." The relief I feel at seeing her lets me know just how much worry I had over all of my crew being dead. "Are there others? Who else survived?"

She shakes her head. "Many. Not that you cared about us. Only the mission. We were just a means to an end for you."

I want to scream that it was because I cared about my crew so much and protecting our dreams for exploration that

I was so strict. But that's not what she wants to hear.

My voice catches. "I—I care about all of you. Truly. Please believe—I've been desperate to find you. To know that some of you, any of you are alive…" I swallow, so weak I have to clench my emotions in my throat. "I'm grateful you're alive, Leinita."

Her expression softens like she believes me. "I'll get the others." She ducks through the door of the temporary metal shelter where I hear other women's voices outside.

"Wait!" I shout, but she doesn't hear.

I don't get to ask about Oten, where he is, if he's okay. What happened to us.

My head floats with nausea, and I roll to my back.

I don't understand why I care so much—about Oten, about my crew. I don't get emotional, ever, and I'm having to choke back tears. I can't be attached to anyone. I have a mission. I have a duty. I have to deal with a huge crisis: a crew with no ship. And no ally for rescue.

Dr. Leinita is female. That's a surprise. I didn't know, but I'm elated. I assumed most of my crew was male. Which was partly why I kept the regulation of everyone wearing their shellskin armor, helms, and voice scramblers at all times.

I didn't want snap judgments about each other's differences—gender, beauty, race, speech—to interfere with our work.

My right-hand lieutenant, Jens, whose real name she said was Jenie, revealed herself to me and asked me to lift the regulation. She maintained the crew needed to exist as individuals in order to work better together.

I abolished the unfair Ten Systems' regulations—corporal punishments, torture, imprisonment for infractions—the barbaric and inhumane things. But I didn't want to change too much and cause chaos among the new crew. I stuck to as many of the humane regulations as I could.

I chastised Jenie for breaking protocol and revealing herself to me, without administering the abusive punishment the regulation called for the infraction. Because I'd abolished the punishment was why Jenie felt safe coming forward in the first place.

Perhaps I was harsh, though. I didn't tell her I was female.

We were on the run, desperate for our lives, racing away from the Ten Systems' fleet. I feared any rift or sudden changes would compromise us.

I assume that's what Dr. Leinita doesn't approve of.

But even as I sit, forced to face the anxiety I feel in being connected as I am to my crew, I wonder if that's the real reason I kept the one-gender regulation. If I didn't know who they were as individuals, I never had to worry about growing attached to them. I didn't have to worry about the pain and loss of losing them—like I experienced with my parents—if I never knew my crew personally.

Other female voices sound from outside. One shrieks in surprise, "General Nem is female?"

I cringe and roll over in bed, facing the wall.

They're alive, so many of them. Even if they are rebelling against me, I'd rather that than have them dead.

"We found her with a Ssedez," another voice says.

There's a hard gasp. "Did she—?"

The voices drop to a low level that I can't understand.

I cover my face in my hands. The way they must have found us... Naked, countless spots of Oten's semen all over the cave floor, both of us chafed from too much sex.

Shame isn't something I feel. I made the choice to have sex with Oten as a preferable alternative to the pain and delirium.

I wanted to be seen with him. The kind of pleasure I experienced with him is something everyone should have. Since I took off my armor and got to be myself for the first time in decades, I want to be known this way. To be the feminine sexual being I am and for everyone to know it.

I understand now how inhumane it was to force us to hide in armor.

I didn't know how important it was to be seen. Until now.

I reveled in sex with Oten for more reasons than to relieve my bodily misery. The desire toxin in the air doesn't explain the trust I grew to have in him. He could have treated me much differently. If he had been someone else, someone less honorable or respectful, it wouldn't have mattered the pain, I never would've touched him.

My crew don't need to know that though.

They'll understand. They will have felt the...

Wait.

It's gone.

I don't feel it—the burn—for the first time in days.

It's like floating in water after days of being enflamed.

My body is mine again.

I have other discomforts. I reach between my legs and wince on contact. I am so sore, it's impossible for me to put my legs together.

I don't think I'll want to have sex again for the rest of my life.

Two other women enter, one I recognize as my number one.

"Lieutenant General Jens," I say, unable not to smile. She's alive! I try to sit.

"Please. Lie down. Rest," she says in an even voice. Her expression is cool, disciplined, but not harsh. Her brown hair is pulled back in a braided crown that rests at the nape of her neck. She kept her hair long, despite needing to keep it wrapped up inside her helm every day.

The other woman has short hair like mine.

So many female members of my crew—how did I not

notice? No wonder they're angry with me.

"It's Jenie, by the way. I'm not Jens anymore." She gives a crack to her neck, and her jaw hardens into a sharp line. "The surviving officers and I voted on some new policies in your absence."

"Voted?" It was always a chain of command, all orders to be followed. "I don't understand. There is no democracy in the military."

The other woman by her ranking insignia could be one of a dozen lieutenants among my officers. "We're not in the military anymore, Nem. We escaped to get away from it."

My confusion must be obvious, because Jenie puts a gentle hand on my arm. "We're in this for research and discovery. You got us away from the Ten Systems. Now it's time to let that all go."

Tears well in my eyes. If I weren't so weak I could contain them, but in my vulnerable state, I can't stop them. But I'm too full of elated surprise to care.

What I've realized over the last few days with Oten, being myself, not disguising who I am or what I desire, the way I haven't since…before I enlisted at fifteen, is I need that. We need that, to be free and not have to hide ourselves. To have our opinions be heard and acknowledged as equal. For everyone to have a say in our mission forward.

I try to keep my lip from quivering and fail. "You're right. We don't have to do the things the Ten Systems forced us to anymore. We should be free to be ourselves."

Both women let out a sigh of relief, and Jenie's mouth bends in a smile. I realize now how worried they were about me disapproving of their decisions.

I clasp Jenie's hand. "You are in charge without me here. The situation required changes. I respect your choices."

"If we'd known you were alive, we would've waited," she offers. "You should know that."

"We want to follow you," says the other woman. "You are the center of all of us. Without you, we would still be enslaved to the Ten Systems' empirical regime."

I'd never thought of it that way. "I guess we were enslaved to them, weren't we?"

"We had no choice," Jenie says. "They forced us to be there on pain of death."

I'm desperate to know about the rest of the crew. "Did everyone survive?"

"Not all," Jenie says carefully, though she doesn't offer the names of who are among the missing. "But our numbers are above five hundred, and more trail into camp from the scattered escape pods every day."

It's more survivors than I expected, but five hundred among a crew of over a thousand still leaves too many casualties. So many dead.

I'm too afraid to ask the names. Too raw to endure the grief.

I wipe the tears from my face as best I can and try to control my voice through the hoarseness. "I'm Nemona."

Both women give me broad smiles.

"General Nemona," the woman beside Jenie says, "I'm Lieutenant Uhlah."

I smile back at her. She was "Uhl" before, my naysayer, the soldier who invaluably questioned my every decision. Often to my annoyance but always helping me see more options. "It's good to see you."

Jenie nods her approval. "We should speak alone."

Uhlah gives me one nod of acknowledgment then leaves.

Jenie pulls a chair up beside my bed. "You have no idea how relieved I am."

"I'm grateful you did what needed to be done."

She tilts her head. "I'm glad you're back."

I have to ask. "Any chance you were able to salvage—"

"We have all of Dr. Klearuh's research files intact."

I breathe for what feels like the first time in days. "How have you combatted the desire component of this place? Did you give me an antidote?"

"We created one with the ship's still-functioning medical systems. As soon as we got our homing device functioning, it picked up your computer's signal. We followed the path around the cliff side to the cave and gave you the antidote as soon as we found you."

I look away, unwilling to hear more about what she saw. "And Oten?"

"The Ssedez?"

"Was he administered the antidote as well?"

Her eyes narrow with confusion. "No. Why would we?"

"Why wouldn't you?" I gasp in horror. "How long has it been?"

"He is surviving. We have him chained and—"

"As if chains will work on him," I rage. "You can't just leave him burning and alone."

"Yes, we can." She stiffens away from me. "Nemona, you were forced to have sex with him for days. How can you care about what happens to him?"

I shake my head so hard it hurts my neck. "No. I was not forced. He did nothing I didn't ask him to do."

"You only asked because there was no one else to relieve you."

I can't agree with her. The thought of lying contorts my stomach. "I chose him because I wanted him."

She recoils from me then checks herself. "I'm sorry. I don't judge you for your choices. But I would not have done the same."

"I would make the same choice again." And what a pleasurable choice it was. I have no regrets, none, no matter how she disagrees with my decisions.

She holds up her hands in a peace offering. "I concede, I only went twelve hours without the antidote, and I was in an escape pod with two other female crew members and, well..." She smiles. "Let's just say, we took care of each other very well."

"I did the same as you."

She leans on her knees. "It is not the same. You were compelled to have sex with the enemy who attacked us without warning or provocation! They destroyed our ship and killed members of your crew!" The horror in her voice makes it sound like sex with Oten was some form of torture.

Well, it was, but not in a bad way. Until the end at least. But that wasn't because of Oten. That was the damn cloud we climbed into. "I only did what I wanted to do."

"You can't possibly have *wanted* to do it with him!" She's outraged, and I've offended her.

I arch up in the bed. "I hadn't had sex with anyone in ten years. Ten years, Jenie!" I fall back, exhausted from my outburst.

She gasps. "No one?"

"I didn't know how badly I needed it. He didn't hurt me. He helped me." At least, that's a believable reason for why I would do it. Though I know it's not the only reason.

She gazes at the floor and says softly, "I have certain restrictions of my own around celibacy." She meets my eyes. "I understand. And the point is—it's over. He'll never touch you again."

"What if I want him to?" It's out of my mouth before I can think twice about it.

Her stare ices over with bitterness. "Members of our crew are dead because of him. Assura is gone!" Fury rages from her eyes, and she sits forward in her chair.

My heart beats faster but not because of Oten. "Assur...?" My voice of reason, the one person who I could depend on. The operative who was instrumental in gaining us the information we needed to escape and staged a seamless diversion that made it all possible. "She"—I didn't know she was female either—"is dead?"

"Her name was Assura," Jenie nearly spits in my face. "I saw her stabbed in the gut by a Ssedez. I don't know how the knife pierced her armor, but it did. She didn't make it onto any of the escape pods."

"That you know of. She could still be out there."

She shakes her head. "The wound was fatal."

I mourn her loss, but the pain I hear in Jenie's voice sounds worse than mine. "You were close?"

"She…we were lovers. For a time."

My heart clenches, and I stroke her hand, comforting her as best I can. "I will miss her very much, too."

Uhlah sneaks her head in the side of the door. "Some more crew wandered in from the jungle."

"I'm coming," Jenie calls and wipes her eyes. "You concentrate on healing. I'll keep charge until you're well enough to take the reins again." She stands to go.

"Wait," I call to her.

She stops at the door. "Yes?"

"What will happen to Oten?" I ask, trying to keep my voice from betraying my fear.

Jenie straightens her shoulders, and her eyes betray a hardness. "The researchers are combing through Dr. Klearuh's files for a way to execute him. That's what we voted on. I'm sorry, Nemona." She ducks out of the tent.

Horror slams me in the chest.

He can't die. Oten won't die. They'll never find a way to kill him. It's impossible.

But in their war with the Ten Systems a century ago, a huge number of Ssedez were killed. They can die somehow, but it's difficult to kill them.

That thought doesn't stop my heart from racing. I have to get to the files. If there is anything to find, I'll get to it before the others. I know the organization of those files better than anyone.

I try to sit up, to get out of bed, but a bolt of agony shoots from my core up my spine.

Dr. Leinita reenters. "You're not ready to sit up yet." She walks to a cabinet and pulls out an ointment. "I've already applied this to your vulva area twice, but I'm sure you need more."

Oh, that's why I can't sit up.

Literally, too much sex.

She hands me the tube. "Use as much of it as you want. It should heal by tomorrow."

"Tomorrow?" I accept it, grateful. I'll have to be up before that.

I gingerly apply it at first, but there's a cooling, soothing quality to the cream that feels so good, I apply it generously.

I have to get some of this to Oten, and the antidote. Tonight.

Chapter Twenty

OTEN

My lungs are working again. My breathing has returned to normal.

But the burn still rages through me.

I can no longer touch myself. My cock hurts to where if I use it again, I will injure it. There is no relief from the desire flames in my blood.

The only relief is in my mind. I remember her. I lie on the floor of my cage, an iron one that I could break if I had the will. But I cannot move. Let alone escape. Shackles chain my ankles and wrists. I grip the bars of the cage to keep my hands from accidentally reaching for my cock.

And I dream. Of her.

Except, unlike how it has been for the last few days, it's more than just physical.

I dream of fucking her—raw and soul-wrenching in my desperation for her. Her need for me matching mine.

But there's more.

And it's so much worse.

I dream of being with her while not consumed with this forsaken desire. Of having hours of uninterrupted conversation with her where she tells me about her life, everything there is to know about her. And that she wants to know about me and asks me about the life of the Ssedez.

I try to resist, try to shove away those dreams and the longing it fills me with to experience them. I try to drown my thoughts in the sexual ones. But no matter how I force them away, I cannot stop thinking about knowing her—not just physically—but knowing her heart and mind as well.

I imagine her life and what it must have been, up to now. The things she must have learned as a human.

I need to deny this longing in me, to keep myself from feeling this way, to not Attach to her in heart the way I have in body. She is not Ssedez.

But I lose the battle.

I imagine what stories I would tell her of the Ssedez that she does not know, and that she is as fascinated by my stories as she was of the ones she learned from humans.

I imagine her voice, beside me.

"Oten," she whispers in the dark. I open my eyes, hoping to see her face, but there is no light.

She strokes my cheek, and I murmur, "Are you real?"

"Yes." She nudges between my lips with her thumb. "Open your mouth for me. I have something for you."

I do. I will do anything she says.

She puts something on my tongue that releases a cool liquid in my mouth. The taste is vile, and I nearly cough, but she eases my mouth closed. "It will make the burning stop."

If that's true, it's the sweetest thing I have ever tasted.

I feel her hand on my thigh, and I'm afraid she'll touch my cock, which would be the most painful thing she could do to me.

I lift my manacled hands and try to push hers away.

"It's all right," she says. "I have something that will help."

Then I feel something soft and smooth and cool touch my cock. I can't help groaning a loud, low sound. The relief is instant. Whatever it is soothes my overused flesh.

Then, for the first time in far too long, my cock softens, and my erection recedes. My fangs retract into my gums with ease, and the burn subsides, a coolness weaving its way into my veins.

It relaxes me.

She brushes her lips over mine in a featherlight kiss. "I'll come back with more as soon as I can."

I whisper, "Thank you," and fall asleep.

When I wake, there's sunlight streaming through the bars of my cage. By instinct, I retreat from it, expecting the burn to curse me. But nothing comes. Nothing happens.

My body is mine again. With only my feelings.

I glance at my cock, soft and resting against my abdomen. I sigh and laugh a little.

My general brought me relief in the night.

I wonder how long it will last, whatever it is she gave me.

I wonder when she'll come back. If she will come back.

She has to. She came for me once. She will come again. Though now she is among her humans and has her antidote, the only thing to pull her back is if she misses me. If she feels something for me.

Which my instinct says is unlikely.

But why else would she help me?

My goal should be to contact my warriors, to let them know I am alive and where I am. Then I can get back to them and lead them to the vulnerable location of the humans so we can finish them.

But that's all secondary now. I have to know she is safe. I have to be with her.

It rips me in two to realize that being with her is more important than returning to my fellow Ssedez. I cringe against it and search myself.

There has to be a way around this. I have to get back to my mission.

But the Attachment has cemented itself within me. To leave her behind in order to set out on a mission to kill her and destroy everything she's worked for…it is impossible.

I would have to flay myself wide open and cut out my heart to do it. And no matter how badly I want to avenge the family and loved ones who were killed all those decades ago by the Ten Systems—I want General Nem more.

It is the shock of my life. A betrayal of everything that has ever mattered to me. But that is insignificant next to how much I want her.

I cannot dwell on it. It will drive me insane.

I can only act.

I stand and go to the bars of my cage. I see the view for the first time and can hardly believe it's real.

The jungle, the greenery I've become accustomed to on Fyrian is all around, but what's front and center in my view is horrifically sublime.

The starship *Origin* lies at the bottom of a valley. There is carnage—the soil overturned in her wake, thousands of trees uprooted—but she is all in one piece by some miracle. Much will be salvageable in that wreckage, and obviously has been.

Behind my cage, there is a village of emergency shelters set up by Nem's crew.

"You are a large one, aren't you?"

I whip around, expecting to see someone outside my cage but see no one. "Who's there?"

It comes again, low and ethereal. "You're a prisoner, that's obvious. But just how dangerous are you?" The voice moves as it speaks, travels down the side of my cage to the front. It's so near, I can't tell if it's inside my cage.

The voice isn't threatening, but it's still unnerving to have no idea who is speaking.

"Reveal yourself. Who are you?"

"I won't give up my advantage so easily." The quip to the words is playful, the tone rasps in a way a human's wouldn't. I'm guessing it's not a member of the *Origin's* crew. "You first."

I could use an ally, so I'll play nice. "I am Oten, of the Ssedez."

"Ot-TEhn. Ssssssedez." The voice exaggerates my accent as though trying out the words and playing with them. "And you are a leader. I am thinking you must be. But where are your people? These humans share no love with you." The voice floats along the front of my cage as though pacing.

"My people are elsewhere."

"Elsewhere… Is this a place? Me thinks not." It gets closer as though sneaking through the bars of the cage. "Answer the question. Where are you from? What planet?"

"I do not know where my people are now. I will not tell you what planet the Ssedez call home. I would die before I tell you that." We have no desire for the Ten Systems to discover us. No other species but Ssedez can know the planet we call home.

"Why?" The voice jiggles with something that resembles humor. "Dying is a serious thing to do for such a trivial fact."

"The safety of my people is not trivial."

"Who are you in danger of?"

"If you do not know, then I am sorry for you." Whoever this is, I cannot decide if they are cunning or stupid. Stupid, if they do not know the danger of the Ten Systems' fleet.

"We are on the same side then," the voice says with resignation. "I am Koviye of the Fellamana." A face appears, slowly, as though layers of air peel away and reveal, well, I am not certain what I see.

There is a face, eyes, a nose, and mouth, an outline of a neck and a body. The jawlines and arching brow appear masculine. But he's translucent. I can see the trees on the other side through him. I imitate his greeting and accent. "Koviye. Fellamana. Where are your people?"

His mouth curves upward at the corners. "Around. Why are you a captive of the human rebels?"

"Rebels?"

"They are not of the Ten Systems' fleet, that is certain."

"Their ship is Ten Systems. Their uniforms are Ten Systems."

"You do not listen, Ssedez." He lets out a frustrated sound and leans against the bars of my cage. "Their biggest worry is similar to ours. They do not want to be found. They are rebels. Don't you think if they were truly of the fleet, there'd already be a rescue here?"

True. I do not know why I did not think of this. But if Nem was part of a rebellion, she would have told me. I think.

He continues, "I like you. You seem—what's the word?—honoran, norable, blohoran? I learned their language in a week."

"Honorable?" I have spent my life learning their language. You cannot study your enemy if you do not understand how they speak.

"Yes, that one! I will share with you." Koviye becomes corporeal, or as solid as a person can look whose skin has translucent qualities. It's like I can see into him, as though his life's blood is visible, an iridescent blue and purple. A flowing garment covers him, one that has a similar iridescent quality of his skin. The only reason I know it's a garment is because he runs the edges through his fingers.

There's movement nearby and some human voices, but they move away.

"They talk of research," he speaks softly. "Do you know about this? What kind of information would human rebels be after?"

It makes me think of Nem's fascination with my Ssedez stories. "Could they be explorers?" If it is possible, if any of it is true, the mistake I made in attacking their ship—it is catastrophic. It would mean my actions were an act of war against a peaceful mission. No different from the ones the humans took against the Ssedez a century and a half ago.

Koviye's eyes light up, and when I say light up, literal yellow shines from his irises, subtle, not blinding in the daylight. Though at night they would light up a forest. "This would make sense. They have many images of maps, and they are often talking of going somewhere. Though I don't know how." He nods toward the ship wreckage at the bottom of the valley. "Their primary worry is how to get off Fellamana."

"Is that the name of your world?"

"What is your name for our world? Do tell." He moves closer to me like this is delicious information.

"The Ssedez call this place Fyrian. The fire world."

"Ah, yes. The burning. Have you had the human's version of the *topuy?* You do not seem in the throes of the *desidre*."

"No, I am in my own mind again. After days wandering the jungle suffering from the—*desidre*, you call it?"

"Days? Oh, that must have been wonderful. Did you enjoy it? Oh, wait." He grimaces. "Were you alone? I'm sorry."

"I was not alone. But it was not wonderful."

"You lie." A mischief that is clearer than the form of his body tilts the corners of his eyes. "Were you with a human? I bet it *was* ecstatic. I've been watching them. They're so uptight." He gives a shiver as though them being uptight is a seductive quality.

It makes me remember *her*, us, together and…it happens, as I thought it might never again. A warmth floods my groin.

Not an erection, that would still be too painful, but thinking of her, of Nem, of what is was like to be buried in her and fucking her within an inch of her life and with all of mine—it makes me want to do it again.

Unbelievably.

It makes me miss her.

With a longing in my heart that awakens like a fierce dragon—roaring and clawing to get to her—I grab and shake the bars of my cage. "I have to get out of this thing."

"Who?" Koviye stands in front of me, his face next to mine. "Tell me. Which human."

"Their leader," I say, before I should. It's not his business who was my lover in the *desidre*. But I do not want to hide it. She is mine, and I want everyone to know it.

His eyes widen, and an unpleasant twist to his mouth replaces all his jovial remarks with a twinge of bitterness. "The leader? How is it that you have had the very one I've been watching?"

A growl rumbles through my chest. "Stop watching her. Now." *She is mine*, I want to roar. But I do not. That is…not true. Though my heart and body screams that it should be.

He searches my face with eyes that see more than they should. "You're a possessive kind, aren't you, Ssedez? Sorry to tell you, but monogamy and the *desidre* do not go together. Those who are possessive on 'Fyrian,'" he mocks the name, "they die. Don't be one of those, Oten."

"Die? Why would being possessive cause death?"

"The *topuy* you've taken? It feels good now, but it won't relieve all of the *desidre*. Over time, you will develop an immunity to the antidote, and you will have to learn to deal with it." A bit of evil enters his eyes. "Those who try to claim one lover on this planet will lose themselves to jealousy. Having merely one lover while living with the *desidre* is impossible. It will kill you."

Spoken by someone who has never experienced the Ssedez Attachment. "And why would I die? What would kill me?"

"Not what. Who." The look he gives me is brutal possession. Like he's territorial over something. Like he plans to—

I slam against the bars of the cage. "She's mine. Do not touch her!"

He laughs and leaps out of my reach. "Goodbye, Oten." With the flash of a vindictive smile, he disappears.

"Koviye!" I shout. "I'll kill you, motherfucker."

"Oh, *motherfucker*," he imitates the human swear, his voice sliding invisible by my ear.

I swat at him, but touch nothing.

He laughs again, farther away, outside my cage. "Don't kill yourself."

"Koviye!" No answer comes. I shout his name again, but he is gone.

I swear more in my own language. Clouds of anger shroud my thoughts. I have to get to Nem. I cannot let this Fellamana take her from me.

But maybe it is insanity. She is not mine. She would never agree to that. And should not. But the rationale does not change the consuming drive eating me from the inside.

The animal in me, the instinct that has Attached to her, wants to do battle, to fight and prove to Koviye and everyone that I will protect her better than anyone. I will kill anyone who gets in my way.

I could bend the bars of the cage now, break the manacles at my wrists and ankles.

No.

I close my eyes and force myself to breathe. I have heard other Ssedez talk about the irrational behavior the Attachment causes. I have seen it in action. I recognize it.

It still takes every ounce of my strength to control it. I am not an animal. I am a civilized intelligent being.

I will wait until dark then I will find her. There will be fewer humans around. Fewer chances of someone getting hurt. If what Koviye said is true, that these humans are in rebellion, they are my allies, not my enemies.

But Koviye could be lying. I hardly know if he's real. He could be a hallucination.

I have to find Nem. Not just because Koviye is after her. But because I need her.

Because I cannot be away from her.

Because, if I really have committed a horrible crime against her people, I have to make it right.

Chapter Twenty-One

Nemona

It's back.

I heal. It doesn't hurt to sit or walk, and now each time I think of him, I feel it again. The desire compound is affecting me despite the antidote.

Except it's different. It's not a desire to just randomly fuck.

It's a desire for him.

His body, his strength. His touch, his care.

Just him.

Oh, and his huge cock.

I wonder if it's the same for him. The burning lust didn't force him to do nice things for me or satisfy me amidst his own lust.

I found a record in the files, hidden in my grandmother's private journal entries, files only I have access to. The findings are extraordinary.

A century ago during the war between us and the Ssedez,

my grandmother had an affair with a male Ssedez. The irony is thrilling. Perhaps it's in my DNA to find the Ssedez irresistible.

She left a record of her secrets where only I, her granddaughter, would be able to read them someday.

She reveals the one way a Ssedez can be killed in combat. There are other ways, mass-killing ways: fire, explosives, exposure to the vacuum of space. That's how the Ten Systems killed most of them. Those methods are well documented. But none of those are an option against just one. My crew would never burn someone alive, even a Ssedez.

But there is one other method for killing a Ssedez one-on-one.

One only a lover would know. One my grandmother could've only found out from intimate experience.

I never thought about it. The one place Oten's armor peels back. The only place there's a seam in his natural armor, and his soft flesh beneath is exposed: the tip of his cock while aroused.

I encrypt the information, hiding it even deeper, where none of the *Origin* researchers will find it.

I learn other secrets—vital ones that will help me—and him. I send up thanks and gratitude to Dr. Klearuh and her fearless rebelliousness that led her to have an affair with the enemy. It makes me feel a little less crazy.

It makes me more desperate to be with him.

Outside the temporary shelter, it's dark and quiet.

Everyone has gone to bed. I sneak around the backs of the metal shelters toward Oten's prison. No one knows I'm out of the hospital bed, and I want it that way.

Now that my crew has found their newfound democratic

system, I can't disrupt that or go against the decision they made to execute Oten, unless I want to cause a mutiny. But even though as their general I can't order them not to kill him, as the woman who spent days fucking and knowing all the pleasure that he and his glorious body are capable of, I can't let him die.

I'll find a way to convince my crew that we need to reach out to the Ssedez and make peace with them—even attempt to form an alliance against the Ten Systems. But that will take time, and I can't risk them killing Oten between now and then.

From the shadows, an arm shoots out and comes around me. My instinct to defend, to break the arm and punch the face, is quelled by the feel of him—his armored skin.

The caress of the diamond pattern along his forearm is a comfort. I run my hands over his arms, the feel of them so strong, so durable yet smooth and sensitive at the same time.

"It's me," he whispers in my ear, and I turn to him, unable to stop touching his chest, his shoulders.

"They took your weapons." I notice right away when my hands don't touch holsters and the knives that usually crisscross his chest.

"I will find others." He inches his hands around my waist and leans his face down to my neck. He inhales against my skin, his hands roaming my back over my uniform.

In spite of every boundary I should have against expressing it, I murmur, "I missed you."

He moans a sound of pleasure and strokes my cheek. "And I you." He kisses me and holds me. My arms wrap around his neck, my body pressed as close to his as I can. It's not even about desire. It's about wanting to be near him. About the familiarity of his touch, the surety of his presence, and the knowledge that I know above anything else—I trust him.

I thought maybe it was something that was induced by the lust. That I trusted him with my body, for him to give me pleasure. But it's more than that.

"Do you have a plan?" I whisper.

"Step one complete." He sighs in my ear and caresses the back of my head.

"They want to kill you."

"Will you let them?" He thinks I have ultimate control over their actions.

I don't. "We have to talk."

I lead him away from the shelters to the edges of the jungle, out of the reach of the camp lights.

"Is your authority in question?" he assesses in a low voice. There's no judgment in it, so I confess.

"While we were in the woods, they adopted a democratic system that I could never in good conscience undo. It is their right."

His brows scrunch in confusion. "I did not think the Ten Systems knew the concept of democracy."

"They don't. It's long dead. Something from ancient times. But my crew wants to try it. And so do I."

"Even though it means they will try to kill me."

"Yes."

He's silent a moment. I can't see his face in the shadows, and I expect derision, but instead he caresses my cheek. "You are a good leader."

"I should've known this is what they needed sooner, but I learn from my mistakes."

He's quiet a moment then says gently, "What kind of military operation are you? I never asked and should have."

A hope sparks in me. Perhaps he might believe me, now that there's more trust between us. "One that isn't. We're not military anymore." Saying it out loud calms me. We truly escaped the Ten Systems. They still haven't found us.

We're not at war anymore. That's the mistake I made. "We're explorers. Our mission is discovery."

"You didn't tell me." His tone is accusatory.

"You didn't care. You were blind to all but your rightful hatred of us. My grandmother, Dr. Klearuh, was a researcher. She headed an expedition over a century ago to study all the intelligent life in the universe."

He snorts. "Not possible."

"No, but a worthy crusade."

"You expect me to believe humans did this? The same humans who sought genocide against the Ssedez? What were they looking for? More people to conquer?" His indignation pisses me off.

I grab his shoulder. "Those humans who murdered your people are gone. All of them are dead. Humans don't live that long. Revenge against those who wronged you, at this point, is null."

"The Ten Systems is still alive! They would do it again!" He seethes through his teeth.

"And there are those of us who would stop it. We're in rebellion for that reason. We do not prescribe to their credo of conquering the universe."

He pauses, his breath relaxing. "You are explorers, out to discover other forms of intelligent life?"

"Yes."

"Peacefully?"

"Yes." I tap his chest for emphasis.

"If this is true, then I am truly sorry."

I stiffen. "Why?"

"I have committed murder."

Chapter Twenty-Two

Oten

Koviye was right. We invaded her ship without communication, without cause, without justification. Our only reason, a one-hundred-year-old fear of them and long memories of the past.

She's right. There are no humans left alive who helped slaughter the Ssedez.

I ordered my crew to commit a horrendous crime.

I have the urge to push her away. "Why are you standing here?"

She backs up, not touching me. "Why wouldn't I be?"

"I killed members of your crew. You were on a peaceful mission. How can you touch me and speak to me and give me antidotes and—"

"You never thought anything of it before."

"Before, I thought you were a Ten Systems' ship out to make war and conquer. This is entirely different."

"Is it?" Her voice is soft and distant. Like she's gone somewhere but I don't know where. "My crew thinks I should be finding a way to kill you. Are you saying you agree?"

"Yes!" She stares at the ground, and it pains me. "If what you say is true, I have committed a heinous war crime: attacking a peaceful vessel. Why didn't you change your markings? Everything about the *Origin* said warship."

She shrugs her shoulders. "We were military. We escaped the Ten Systems' fleet. We'd only just begun to accept that we'd gotten away. I kept expecting them to find us."

The accomplishment is admirable. "How did you achieve it?"

"Careful planning. Some luck. A great crew. A ruthless desire to do the right thing." She steps closer to me again. "I understand why you did what you did. It wasn't a war crime. You couldn't have known. I should've changed the markings on the *Origin*."

"If we had hailed you, communicated first rather than attacking you, what would you have done?"

There's a smile in her voice, even if I can't see it in the shadow. "We would've wanted to learn anything and everything about the Ssedez that you would share with us. Including and especially your side of the war with the Ten Systems."

Remorse floods me, as hot as the *desidre* before she gave me the *topuy*. "You've gotten your education."

"No, I haven't."

I am bitter. Defensive. "You mean fucking a Ssedez for days wasn't enough?"

"I don't just want to know how you fuck."

"That's not what you said a few days ago when you were on your knees begging to know what a gold cock tasted like."

She reaches out to stroke my arm. "I want to know more. Your stories and your life."

I inhale to argue with her. Everything she's saying goes against every assumption I've had about her species. "You are very different from most humans, Nem."

"There are many more like me." She softens and reaches for my other hand. "There's something I wanted to tell you. I didn't think it was a big deal, but now it feels like it is."

"What?"

"My name. It's not Nem. It's Nemona."

My anger deflates, and I hold her hand tighter. "They forced you to change your name?"

She shrugs. "It didn't seem like anything to give up at the time. Not when I was a teenager and didn't care what it took to become strong enough to fight anyone and everyone who could hurt me."

I stiffen. "Who would hurt you?"

"Who doesn't want to hurt an orphaned child fighting to stay alive on the streets?"

"An orphan? But you said, your grandmother's research—"

"The government took everything from my family when they realized what she found didn't support their goals to dominate the universe. Every study suggested that all intelligent life comes from the same source. It refuted the Ten Systems' assertions that humans are the superior species."

"But that does not explain why your family left you behind."

"My parents died trying to hide me. But I was old enough for them to teach me who my grandmother was before they were gone. Old enough to know where they'd hidden the copies of the files the Ten Systems' government tried to destroy."

It begins to make sense, why she ended up leading a rebellion. "That's why your crew followed you."

"Once word spread of who I was, and what I had in my possession, they backed me."

Then my warriors and I crippled their mission. "Are

there other ships in your rebellion?"

She shakes her head, and her voice is heavy with regret. "The *Origin* is all we have."

"I will help. The Ssedez will help." It's an impulse, but the right one. "We will help repair your ship."

Her brows scrunch with skepticism. "How are you going to convince the Ssedez of that? Your entire existence is about remaining a secret from humans. They'll never agree."

"They follow me. They listen to me." I stand away from the tree, more certain of what I need to do. "I need to get in touch with my ship."

"Even if you convince them to help, your ship won't have everything we need to repair the *Origin*. You destroyed the reactor."

I grasp her shoulders. She doesn't understand how important it is to atone for the crimes we committed against her crew. "I will go back to my planet and bring whatever you need. Once I explain to them what's happened and the mistake we made, they'll want to help, too."

She places her palms on my chest. "I want to believe you, but I can't see how it's possible."

"Let me worry about how. Where are the camp's communication systems so I can contact the Ssedez?"

"They don't have any off-planet communication set up. We're interlinked among ourselves." She points to the commlink device strapped around her wrist. "We're in this fight alone."

A voice comes out of the jungle. "I can help."

It startles Nem—Nemona—and she jerks back, reaching for a weapon in her belt that isn't there. "Who is it?"

"Our technologies are not compatible, so we cannot repair your ship. But we have communications."

I recognize who it is. That ethereal tone, round and resonant, is unmistakable. "Koviye, show yourself."

"I must ask the human a question first." The leaves rustle, and his voice sounds from in front of us. There is no shadow where he is. He remains invisible. "How do I know you won't study my Fellamana like we're things in a museum? What's to keep you from reporting everything you learn back to your Ten Systems?"

Nemona recovers from her surprise. "You live on Fyrian? The Fellamana?"

"Yes." There's a smile in his tone. "You have not heard of us, even in all your studies, have you?"

"No." The curiosity in her voice is apparent, and she relaxes her fight stance. "But I promise, we only want to learn."

"And what will you do with what you learn?"

"Use it for research. Identifying similarities between species of intelligent life. Share it."

"We Fellamana have kept our existence a secret for our own protection. We do not wish the Ten Systems to know we exist."

I'm wondering why he ever revealed himself to us at all, unless... "But you talk to us now. Some part of you wants to connect with another species."

He makes a frustrated sound. "I know everything there is to know about you already."

"I know more about the Ten Systems' military than anyone you'll meet," Nemona says. "I'll share everything I know with you so the Fellamana can better protect themselves. How their tracking systems work so you can fortify yourselves. How their weapons are made so you can be armed against them."

I add, "The Ssedez have spent centuries studying their fighting tactics. We can share what we've learned as well."

"Those are generous offers." His corporeal form begins to show. He is light, as in made of it. I couldn't see it with the sun shining through him this afternoon. His iridescent flesh is matched by the clothing he wears, to where I can't tell where his skin ends and the garment begins, only that it flows over him, hinting at the shape of his body beneath.

"There is attraction between you." He tilts his head curiously at us. "I thought you said their leader was your lover of choice, Ssedez? Or are you possessive of more than one human?"

Nemona inhales a sharp breath and stares at me.

"Who's there?" A woman's voice sounds behind us, her tone threatening.

Nemona and I crouch in the bushes. In the shadows, the woman cannot see us, only hear us.

But Koviye, with his shining figure that doesn't just reflect light but creates it, is visible.

Rather than hide himself like I expect, he steps forward. Or more like glides. He seems to have two legs that contact the ground beneath his garment, but his movements are so fluid, it is hard to decipher his steps beneath his flowing robe.

"Jenie," he says, facing off with the woman. "It is a pleasure."

Jenie stiffens and stares at Koviye in shock. "W-who are you?" she stammers, not lowering her blaster, pointing it at his chest.

"So defensive." Koviye scolds with a click of his tongue. "Is that any way to welcome a stranger?"

She relaxes her aim but doesn't lower her weapon. "Tell me who you are, and I might greet you properly."

He glides closer to her, dangerously close. As close as I might, knowing her blaster won't hurt me. Almost like he's unafraid she could hurt him. "Properly," he muses. "Such a strange word that does not translate into my language. Enlighten me."

He moves to her side as though to circle her.

Jenie stiffens her aim again, following him around her, not letting him behind her. "Properly, as in what's custom."

"Ah, custom. This I know. But I do not think my custom of greeting would please you. Even if you did lower your weapon." He continues his circle around her, forcing her to turn. He's so relaxed, as though mocking her defensive response.

She falls for his bait. "Why wouldn't I like it?"

There's a seductive quality to his movements. Not threatening or one of violence, but he is getting closer to her. "Because my greeting involves touch. And you don't like to be touched, do you, Jenie?"

She keeps her aim, blaster now inches from his chest. "I do not want to hurt you. But if you threaten me, I will."

He pauses in front of her and says in a comforting voice, "Have you met another species before, face-to-face?"

"Yes."

"I mean not in combat. In conversation."

She hesitates. "No."

"A little advice. That." He nods at her blaster. "Is not a good initiation of diplomacy. As far as I know."

Jenie lowers her weapon, slowly, still wary of him. "All right."

He holds out his hand to her. "From what I have observed, this is your custom greeting."

"You've been watching us?"

"That is how I learned your language, yes. Will you shake my hand or no?"

She lifts her non-blaster hand and gingerly rests it in his palm. Her breathing is fast. Her chest moves rapidly in the light from the camp.

Koviye's voice changes. It deepens and thickens. "That's better. May I also greet you with part of the Fellamana custom?"

Her gaze moves over his face warily, but she nods.

He spreads his second hand over her forearm, and a light appears beneath her skin there. "It will surprise you. But I promise it will not hurt."

The light intensifies, and Jenie gasps a sound, like the one Nemona makes when I touch her, when she is about to come. It radiates up her arm and disappears inside her uniform. It reappears at her open collar along her neck then disappears again inside her skull.

She collapses against him. "Stop, please," she murmurs.

He lets her go, slowly, helping her regain her balance. His tone softens with a gentle warning, "You are weak from not feeding the *desidre*."

"I don't need to."

"The *topuy* antidote won't work on you for much longer. You will develop an immunity to it. Don't deny yourself. Take a lover."

She shakes her head, not looking at him. "No." She stumbles backward away from him.

"There is no shame in giving your body what it needs," he says then fades away, drifting once more into invisibility. "At least give yourself release, *lulipah*."

Jenie scrambles for her blaster and runs away.

Chapter Twenty-Three

NEMONA

Jenie retreats to camp, and I have the urge to go after her. The panic on my friend's face makes me want to help her.

"What did you do to her?" I ask Koviye, though I can't see him.

"I showed her how badly she needs to stop resisting the *desidre*. She will become—eh, disease, sick, what is the word?"

"Infected?"

"Yes."

I move to go after her.

Koviye lays an invisible hand on my shoulder. "She will sound the alarm, and you will never get away. Come." The leaves rustle as he moves past and farther into the jungle.

"Why did you reveal yourself to her if you are afraid she will sound an alarm?" Oten asks him.

"She has not had an orgasm in days," he says evenly, as though talking about her eating habits. "She must satisfy herself, or the *desidre* will eat her alive. No matter how much *topuy* she takes."

"Top-pew-ee?" I glance at Oten.

"The antidote that fights the desire lust—that they call the *desidre*."

"De-zee-druh?"

"Yeah."

I glance back at Koviye. "It doesn't work?"

"It eventually loses its effect. You have to feed the *desidre* so you grow used to it. Your body will adjust over time till it is manageable. But it is like any hunger in the body. It must be fed, or you will lose strength."

"But how did you know she hasn't been—feeding the *desidre*?" I ask Koviye, disturbed that he could know this about Jenie and frighten her like he did. "Have you been stalking her?"

"Can't you read it in her body?" he asks with surprise. "The color of her blood beneath her skin, it's tinged with a buildup of the toxin. If she doesn't release it soon, it will sicken her."

"You can see her blood?" Oten asks, as disbelieving as I am.

"Can you not?" Koviye asks just as surprised.

"No," Oten and I answer.

Koviye smiles, as intrigued by our simultaneous response as by the answer. "Interesting. We have much to learn from one another. Follow me." He turns away from us and moves through the jungle, the light of his body showing us the path.

"I guess he's taking us to his leaders?" I ask Oten in a low voice.

"I want to follow him." Oten glances at me, and in the light shining from Koviye, I see Oten's face for the first time in days.

It hits me like a slug to the chest. His wide cheekbones

and his sharp jaw. I want to kiss him.

And I do.

I cup his cheek and reach up on tiptoe. He meets me, bending his mouth to mine.

And it's like no time has passed, like no *topuy* ever entered my bloodstream.

My need for him is an undeniable force inside me. My body responds to him. The desire for his touch, the familiarity of it, the memory of it, of all the glorious things he did to me and made me feel.

His long tongue sweeps into my mouth and wraps around mine in a fierce tug, pulling my tongue into his mouth for him to suck. It's like he is sucking my desire out of me into him, trying to awaken it.

He doesn't know—he needs to do no awakening. I am here for him.

He hugs my back, drawing me against him. "I did not know if you would still want me without the—"

"Yes." I sink fingers into his hair and pull his mouth back to mine. But I feel the tips of his fangs, pressing behind his lips.

I pull back and wipe my mouth, on instinct. I didn't taste any of his venom, but I don't want to risk it.

"I'm sorry," he says, and covers his mouth, too. "You surprised me. I didn't prepare myself."

It all comes flooding back. I may want to save him from dying—but that's all this is. He's dangerous to be kissing at all. He could bite me and turn me Ssedez again, on purpose or by accident.

And my attachment to him, this emotional need that wells up inside me when I'm near him, it has to stop.

Now.

It doesn't mean we can't still fuck.

But that's all this is. My compassion for him begins and

ends with keeping him from being executed. He is nothing more to me than a fascinating alien who is very talented at making me come.

I will maintain a relationship with him suitable for establishing an alliance with the Ssedez. And while we are on Fyrian, we will feed our *desidre* together. That is all.

I box up my other feelings toward him and stuff them where I stuff everything that gets in my way—behind my will for control.

I step back from him and say clinically, "I discovered something in the research about you."

"About me?" He stiffens, startled.

"Nothing bad. Well, just that my grandmother had an affair with a Ssedez."

"Your grandmother?" His eyes widen in shock. "We have no record of a Ssedez having relations with a human. I would know if it were true."

"Which of your warriors would admit to having sex with your worst enemy?"

"They would never lie to me."

"But they would withhold the truth if it meant protecting the person they loved."

His expression softens. "They were in love?"

"She knew very intimate secrets that I can't imagine a Ssedez would reveal to anyone he didn't trust implicitly. So they were at least attached to each other. Intimately."

"What secrets?" His jaw tightens. He's afraid I discovered how to kill him. It's there in his eyes.

I put my palms on his chest. "Secrets I won't tell a soul. Ones that I hid in the database so no other human could find them."

His eyes move over my face, searching me. "Why would you do that?"

"Because..." It's forming in my thoughts, the feelings, the

things he awakens in me that are more than desire. The true meaning behind the trust I have in him.

But I'm not thinking about that.

Thankfully, I don't have to answer him, either.

Koviye's voice interrupts us. "I know a hidden place we can stop in a short while to feed the *desidre*. You've both gone too long without satisfying it."

I step back from Oten, trying to envision Koviye facilitating a scheduled stop in our journey just to have sex.

"You have both fed yourselves today," he says. "But doing so with someone else relieves the toxin for longer."

I glance at Oten with eyebrows raised. Apparently, both of us are healed well enough that we're capable of orgasming without pain. It has me envisioning us together again: of him pouring his hunger into my mouth, unleashing his passion and fucking me so far into oblivion I don't care about my name—only his.

But it also makes me doubt again. Is what I'm feeling for him a mere manifestation of the *desidre* still within me in a smaller dose?

I don't want it to be. I want it to be a desire I have for him, because it's mine.

I see the same fear in his eyes. The stress of worrying over our bodies not being our own.

Koviye must see it, too. "The *desidre* only magnifies what you already feel. For instance, do either of you desire me?"

I think about it a moment. Koviye is fascinating, and what of his body I see beneath his translucent robe is strong and attractive. He would be an excellent lay. That is clear.

But I don't crave him—not the way I do Oten.

"If I am wrong, I would join you." He mouth tilts with a hint of mischief. "It's days since I've had more than my own hand."

"No!" Oten barks.

Koviye shakes his head. "Keep that possessiveness to yourself once you're among the Fellamana. They will delight in teaching you a lesson not to own a person."

"What if I don't want anyone but him?" I say.

Oten's gaze whips to mine. "Truly?" His expression goes from shock to lust to…something so intense and emotionally stirring, I have to look away.

I shrug, trying to make light of my comment. "We're physically compatible. If I have to feed the *desidre*, it may as well be with you."

He growls a predatory sound. "Compatible?"

I glance at him, and if his eyes could throw flames, I'd be burning.

He closes in on me, using his size, the enormity of his chest to get in my space. "You call this"—he motions between us—"compatible?"

My heart races. Having him so close makes me want to grab him, throw him down, and ride him and his divine cock until I'm sore all over again. A little more intense than compatible, I guess.

Koviye laughs low. "Perhaps you two would rather stay here than come with me."

"I have to communicate with the Ssedez," Oten says. "We must repair the *Origin*."

Koviye nods. "Then we'll have to stop, so you can feed the *desidre* before we reach the Fellamana." He turns and continues through the jungle, intending us to follow.

"Come along," Oten says to me. "Your crew is okay without you for now. You can communicate with them from the Fellamana settlement." He points to the commlink on my wrist.

I search for something to say, some reason why I shouldn't go. But leaving him, saying goodbye to him, feels impossible. I glance at him in shock at myself. "I can't leave you."

It doesn't matter that my obligation is to my crew and that I should be here to lead them. I want to go with him.

He raises his eyebrows. "Can you not?" He tucks his chin, his gaze masked and unreadable, like he's hiding something.

I fight the urge to grasp his hand and say, *I want to know you and everything about you.* Instead, I say, "It's part of our mission to learn about new species like the Fellamana. And I didn't get to ask you more about the Ssedez while in the throes of the *desidre*."

"Let's travel while you learn, okay?" Koviye calls, and his light moves away from us.

We follow Koviye into the jungle, and I talk myself down from my guilt for leaving my crew. Jenie is more than capable in charge. And establishing relationships with the Ssedez and the Fellamana are vital to our mission.

Oten takes a deep breath. "Would you like to hear some tales while we walk?"

"Would I!" I say too loudly.

"Shhh!" Koviye flings back at us. "Keep your voices low. There are beasts we don't want to wake."

Remembering our encounter with the *bureuh*, Oten whispers, "I would tell you how we managed the escape that ended our war with the humans."

My breath catches, but I keep walking. "How?"

"A transport. We have the technology to move from place to place."

"Aboard a vessel?"

"No. As in our molecules transferred from one ship to another without a vehicle. We call it Retracting."

I'm having trouble envisioning this. "So when you flew your ship into the middle of the Ten Systems' fleet and it exploded, you weren't aboard the ship."

"We Retracted off of it to another ship."

I've heard rumors of such technology but never seen it,

and I realize how he tricked me before. "It's how you got aboard the *Origin*, isn't it? I thought you said there was a traitor among my crew."

"The traitor was your computer. We hacked into it to allow us to Retract from our ship onto yours."

I have a burst of laughter. "You played me. Led me to believe it was a person."

"We were enemies then."

"And we're not now?"

"You and I are allies. Soon, my Ssedez will know it. And soon we will convince your crew when we supply parts to repair your ship."

I get a chill over my skin. It could work. We might have our first ally in our rebellion against the Ten Systems. "Tell me more."

His stories are mostly war stories, but he mentions family, friends, and people he holds with great affection. I ask about where they are now, and he pauses with heavy silence.

"They died in the war with the Ten Systems?" I don't want it to be true, but of course it is.

"Yes." He changes the subject to lighter things, about the family he still has living. About nieces and nephews born and grown. Watching them—male and female—grow into warriors he has trained and loves.

"How old are you?" I ask.

"I am two hundred and seven years, by the human measurement. Which for a Ssedez, is young."

I snort. "Considering you live forever."

"Not quite."

I slow in my steps. "You don't?"

"A thousand years is about our expected lifespan."

I have to work to keep my words quiet and contain my annoyance. "You let me think you were immortal, outside of a catastrophic event."

"We weren't exactly being honest with each other. You told me nothing of your rebellion."

"True." There were a lot of things we kept to ourselves.

"How old are you?"

"Thirty-two."

"Your human lifespan is about one hundred years?"

"That's about all our DNA will support. Yeah." It's almost eerie how much he knows about humans. "You've studied humans a lot."

"We learn everything there is to know about our enemy."

"Including our language."

"Every warrior learns it in order to study our recordings of your intercepted audio and video transmissions." He pauses, and we listen to our feet crunch through the path of fallen leaves on the jungle floor. "We are a similar age, you know."

I almost laugh. "Um, no."

"In terms of our development, we are comparably between twenty and thirty percent through our lives. You are older actually."

"Except when you're thirty percent through, I'll be dead." I can't conceal my jealousy. To live for a thousand years…to know I had seven more of my lifetimes to live…

I might be able to see the destruction of the Ten Systems' regime. The scope of the empire is too large to topple in my lifetime. But in Oten's life, it could be done.

He's quiet after that, and I search for something else to say to get him talking.

A thought occurs to me. One that worries me but only seems logical for someone who's lived so long. "Do you have a family of your own?" If he has a wife at home, I'll—I don't know.

Feel bad? Jealous? Angry?

To my relief, he says, "No."

"Have you ever?" I ask tentatively, wondering if he lost them in the war.

"No, never."

I wonder if the Ssedez military is similar to the Ten Systems. "Is it a requirement of your warrior's life? To give up having a family?"

"There are many warriors with families."

"Then how come—"

"I never formed the Attachment with anyone." He says the word "attachment" like it has weight, some severity.

"You've never loved someone?" I can't believe that's true.

"I have loved many. But the Attachment is more. Necessary for the Ssedez to reproduce. A meeting of both fate and biology that cannot be forced. It has to occur naturally. This I have never experienced till…" He stops himself, and I'm too curious not to ask.

"Until…?"

He doesn't answer, and it's almost implied by the weight of his silence.

I almost stop walking it hits me so hard. "Until Fyrian?" I whisper.

"Yes," he whispers back.

My heart skips. It seems impossible that after how many centuries of never finding someone that he would feel… "Because of the *desidre*?" That must be it. He can't be feeling this Attachment for me, a human, when he never felt it among his own people.

"Perhaps," he says quietly. His word choice is telling. He knows my language well enough to know the difference between probably, most likely, I think so, and…*perhaps*. The word has such significance, he may as well be saying, *No, it's because of you.*

I remember what I read about his venom, the fangs, about how the appearance of them indicated a "particular attachment on the part of the Ssedez." It never occurred to me that *Attachment* could mean more than attraction.

Maybe the Ssedez never told Dr. Klearuh. Or maybe they left it out.

"I'm incapable of having children," I say, keeping my voice low so Koviye shouldn't hear me.

"Oh?" There's a stiffness, in his tone, like he's not sure if he's allowed to ask more.

"It was a commitment required of joining the military service. No reproduction. I'm bioengineered infertile." I'd never thought of it much. It was a choice I made out of necessity at fifteen. Regretting it is a waste of energy. My life is not conducive to having a family. I know this.

"They forced you?" he asks.

"I chose it."

"But how old were you?"

"It doesn't matter."

He doesn't say anything for a time, and I'm glad. If he tried saying something like *I'm sorry*, I'd punch him. But I feel the sadness radiating off him.

"It is barbaric to require that of soldiers," he says finally.

I shrug. "It's done. Being angry about it helps nothing." In the silence, I think of something I have to say. The way he talks of his family, of raising young warriors—he wants children. "So even if you are feeling this *Attachment,* as you call it, for me—you do not want me."

As soon as I say it, I want to take it back. I just implied that his Attachment to me could actually potentially happen. That we could possibly be something together.

Which is impossible.

I don't want that.

I want no one. I need no one. He is a means to a goal, a source of physical satisfaction. Nothing more. Ever.

"What I mean is," I blurt to correct my error. "All of us,

my entire crew, are infertile. So don't get any ideas about us being possible—you know, mates for your Attachment or whatever."

He rushes up behind me and holds my arm. "Koviye, we're stopping." He leads me into a copse of trees out of reach of Koviye's light. He stops by the dark shadow of a large rock.

"Don't tell me what I want," he whispers with an angry bite. "You have no idea what I want."

My heart pounds against my sternum. "Do *you* know what you want?"

There's a hesitation from him, but he inhales and whispers, "I want you."

I have trouble getting breath into my lungs. The tightness through my chest is a cement block of disbelief. He can't mean what I'm hearing. "No."

The same way I need no one, no one needs me. As much as my crew depends on me, they have all the information. They are capable. I am replaceable.

I am a vital part of no one's life. And that's how it should be. Personal relationships only get in the way of the important things and goals. There's no time for the pain and hurt that comes inevitably from losing someone one loves.

Best to just avoid attachment, capital A or small, completely. It saves everyone and everything.

When Oten says he wants me, he just means physically. He wants me to fuck. The same way I do. That's all.

I'm reading too much in his tone.

His indrawn breath catches and stops as though it hurts. "You do not believe me?" He strokes his arms around my back.

"This is sex, Oten. That's all."

He growls a sound that could be a denial, but I ignore him and push on.

"I don't want to hear any more about your Attachment

thing. It has nothing to do with me. You—"

He kisses me—molding his mouth to mine—stopping my words. His lips possess mine, and the firmness of them, they are unmovable. Soft but unyielding. He traces my lips with his tongue, and once I open my mouth, he is thorough.

And I don't give a shit about who means what to whom anymore.

There is only what he makes me feel.

He licks every inch of my tongue. I try to tangle his with mine, but he takes over, sketching the intricacies of my mouth with those twin tips of his.

Stars could exist in his kisses—the infinite fire, the blinding light, the unquenchable heat. His mouth is all those things.

But if his mouth is the star, his hands orbit around me. They stroke my breasts through my uniform; they clench my hips and grip my ass. And his body...

It is the force, the gravity that holds all of us—him and me and this passion we ride. His body keeps us in one piece.

His mouth leaves mine for my neck, and I get to say, "I learned something else in my study."

He cups my nape, his fingers sliding into my hair. "What?"

"It's something I know you want."

He groans and bites my ear. "Tell me."

I trace the gold muscles of his pecs and down his abs. "It's something I want, too."

He whispers his lips over mine. "Say it."

"I figured out what caused me to turn."

His grip tightens on my neck, and his voice grates. "How?" The reminder is there, the way we couldn't allow him to come in me. The way we didn't know which it was, his venom or his come that made me turn Ssedez.

"It's your venom." I glide my hand below his waist and find his cock. I groan at the feel of it, hard and filling my hand with barely a touch. At the brush of the spirals lining the surface from base to tip. And the memory of what those ridges feel like sliding in and out of me, stimulating my tissues in the most intimate of places.

I don't think I truly appreciated it before. I was too caught in the throes of the *desidre* to notice what a work of art he is—the rigidity and shape of his cock, the finite texture and impressive length…and girth.

He runs his lips across my jaw and murmurs, "What are you saying?"

I pull his head down. "You can come in me."

A growl echoes in his chest.

I wrench my fingers in his hair and crush his mouth to mine.

He hauls me against him, his hands greedy over my ass, his cock rubbing against me. His fangs don't protrude this time. I press his mouth as hard as I can, delving my tongue as deep into him as I can go.

My tongue feels unwieldy. I miss the dexterity of my long, flexible Ssedez tongue, where I could tangle it with his and snake into his mouth as far as I wanted.

But he strokes my thick human tongue like he can't get enough of it. Like it doesn't matter as long as it's mine.

He slides his hand down the front of me, between my thighs. "Are you still sore?"

"No." I press his hand to me harder, easing the ache that's burning there. He obliges, massaging me.

But there's something else I want. I unzip his pants and let his cock out into my hand.

I bite down on his tongue, drawing it out between my teeth, then sink to my knees in front of him.

I've been thinking about putting his cock in my mouth for days. Wishing for the taste of his come sliding down my throat. But I don't want that if he won't be able to come while he's fucking me, too.

"Nemona," he groans my name and slides his hands into my hair.

I stroke him. "Can you orgasm more than once even though I gave you the *topuy*?"

He answers with a deep growl, "I can come as many times as you want."

A dim light, comes from our left. It grows brighter until I can see Oten and all of his erotic glory.

I glance to see the light radiating from Koviye, who stands leaning against a tree with his back to us.

"I thought you might like to see each other," he says, not looking over his shoulder.

Koviye's light touches the broad expanse of Oten's chest, the beauty of him gleaming gold, and my eyes can't help drifting down to his cock, protruding fiercely and fully erect. It makes my mouth water even more.

I see his gaze. It is as hot as I feel. I am pulsing and throbbing between my legs, soaking the undersuit of my uniform.

"Leave the light on," Oten says not taking his eyes from me. "But you cannot watch."

"Done," Koviye says, and it's like he's not even there, except for his glow.

Oten parts the zipper of my uniform and reveals my nipples. The night air caresses me, and the relief from the confinement of my jacket has me arching my back, beckoning him to touch my nipples.

He drags the jacket from my arms and drops it to the ground, his gaze heavy over my breasts, caught in Koviye's light.

I wrap my hand around the hard length of his cock. "Mine," I declare with a smile and drop to my knees.

I place Oten's cock on my tongue and, for a moment,

lose myself in the sensation of the tip of him. The pleasure of feeling his cock in my mouth again, stretching my jaw open and wide. The texture of the ribs around his cock stroking inside my mouth.

Oten gasps, and I look up at him.

I descend, swallowing as much of him to the back of my throat as I can manage.

Oten strokes my cheeks, bringing my attention back to him. "Make me come," he says. "I want you to taste me."

I do. I move my mouth up and down, pulling him in and out of my mouth, feeling him press into my throat over and over. His fingers tighten in my hair, scratching at my scalp, moving my head but too frantic to keep a rhythm. I keep it for him.

The armor at the tip of his cock peels back. The sensitive flesh, the only soft place on him, is tantalizing. I swirl the tip of my tongue over it, tracing the edges of his skin as it retreats.

He cries out with each circle of my tongue, and I know I've found the right spot.

I remember what I learned, how this is the only place he is vulnerable. I'll keep it hidden inside my mouth. Just in case Koviye is peeking.

I grip Oten's ass with my hands and let his hips thrust into my mouth.

The muscles in his ass clench and contract with each move. He roars a harsh animal sound, his thrusts jerking and tightening, and he climaxes.

His thick sensuous come pumps into my throat in delicious bursts. It's a pleasure to swallow, rich and satisfying. It streams into my belly, and it blooms in me like power.

Chapter Twenty-Four

Oten

Her mouth is a haven. Her tongue circles the tender flesh beneath my armor with such sensitivity, it undoes me.

I come hard, claiming the back of her throat, filling her with my essence.

It is only the second time I've come in her mouth. Though it is the thousandth time I have wanted to. She swallows hard and sucks even harder, draining me of every drop. She watches me, her wide eyes declaring how much she loves it.

I glance at Koviye, to make sure he is still not watching. The light from his back glows stronger, as though it's activated by growing desire. I urge Nemona to her feet. I grab her discarded uniform jacket and place it over the boulder.

Her breathing is heavy, and I slide her pants down her legs. Her inner thighs are already damp. I can't help tracing the dampness with my fingers—wanting it on my tongue, on my cock, all at once.

She sits on the rock and spreads her legs. Koviye's rays

move down Nemona's naked body until all of her is visible, even her glistening cunt.

She leans back on her hands, and I slip my fingers into her folds.

I glance at her face, and her panting mouth.

"You're soaking," my voice rumbles.

She lifts her heel to the rock and widens her knees. She opens herself, exposing more of her to me. "Make me wetter."

I kneel in front of her and bury my face between her thighs. The warmth of her against my mouth, on my cheeks. With the taste of her on my tongue, my fangs are aching, pulsing in my gums, but I keep them sheathed—by force of will.

I snake my tongue into all her crevices, exploring and searching, probing through her depths. She puts both her feet on the rock, spreading her knees. I hold her inner thighs wide with my hands, wanting access to every tiny space within her.

I want all of her to be mine.

She grips my head and arches her hips into me. I hum against her and sink my tongue deeper. I circle the twin tips of my tongue over the rounded spot inside her, and she cries out.

I use my fingers to pull her wetness backward and press my finger to the pucker of her ass. She bucks against my mouth. "More."

She opens for me, and I slip my wet finger, slowly into her ass—the lube dripping from her easing the way.

Her ragged moan vibrates all the way down her body, and she relaxes, letting me deeper.

"Yes!" she screams then grits her teeth.

And comes.

She convulses, her thighs shaking, her cunt spasming around my tongue, her body clenching my finger. Her orgasmic sounds and rhythms are more pleasing than my own.

I expect her to need a moment to recover, but instead, she grabs my shoulder and pulls me to standing.

She grabs my cock. "Fuck me."

Her arms shake, supporting her, and we watch my cock sink into her wet cunt. My gold spirals disappearing into her pink pussy. Her folds stretch—widening and dripping onto me. She welcomes my invasion, gripping me all the way in.

She throws her head back and moans. The glow of Koviye's light crowns her head and brightens her skin. She stares at where our bodies meet.

I thrust into her, the force shaking her body. Her solid muscle is too hard to shake with my drives, except her breasts.

She thrashes and fixates on my cock, diving in and out of her.

I circle her clit with my thumb, and she starts to come, her hips arching and tightening.

Another sensation comes. One I've not felt before.

The light intensifies until it's blinding, whiting out everything—the jungle disappears, the darkness disappears—and there is only Nemona.

The light spreads to her body, as though it slips beneath her skin, up her spine, but also down. Into her belly, to the apex of her thighs and…

It hits her clit first, and the swollen nub leaps beneath my thumb. She screams, her whole body tensing so hard, I fear she's in pain.

But I don't have time to wonder.

It bolts into my cock within her, and the ecstasy is so intense, I nearly collapse.

It reaches into me, awakens a storm of bliss inside me that consumes me. The light permeates through me, as though healing and cleansing me at the same time. It lights every nerve ending in my body with pleasure.

It lasts for minutes, waving on and on, until I can't remember what's happening or why or how. Only that I am inside Nemona and that she is feeling this with me.

The light connects me to her, and I feel her pleasure, too. It starts a loop, where her orgasm feeds mine and mine feeds hers until she is as much a part of me as myself. As though not just my cock is inside her, but my mind as well.

I feel her, her thoughts, her emotions.

The things she feels—the joy and the warmth. The happiness and the—

Connection, is the only word I dare give it. She feels a connection to me, and it bathes me in a sensation of trust. She trusts me. Wholly. With her life.

She respects me completely, with her intuition.

Her curiosity about me—her desire to know me and learn who I am—occupies the front of her mind.

I realize my eyes are open and so are hers. And I am looking in hers, and she is looking in mine. And we are one.

She is inside of me, seeing all of me, feeling all of my feelings. I can no longer hide it. I am exposed.

But I want to be.

I want her to know everything she means to me. How I return her trust and her respect and curiosity and—

There is more. More that I feel. Words I dare not think.

But I know she feels the feelings within me. I feel her luxuriate in them and wrap them around herself.

I hold her against me, arms around her, never wanting to let her go.

Koviye stands off to the side, his light dim. He's breathing heavily and leaning against a tree. I have the urge to swear at him. For intervening. His light did something to us.

But I can't break this moment with Nemona. I close my eyes again. It's just her and me. Feeling each other.

"The Attachment," she murmurs against my chest. "It's for life."

I hold my breath. She felt that, too. Of course she did.

"Yes," I murmur against her hair.

She leans her head back and looks in my eyes. "And you feel it for me. It's not just the *desidre*." She says it with more certainty than even I had admitted to myself.

I hover my mouth over hers. I will not answer her. The weight of my Attachment will frighten her. I can see it in her eyes—I have never seen her afraid.

She is now.

But if I am honest, my terror matches hers.

It is almost complete. The Attachment. My heart—my feelings—without my knowing, have followed my body and merged with my physical need for her.

The feeling of wholeness merges in my gut and fuses together. It's a feeling of pleasure, of ultimate contentment. I have craved this sensation my whole life.

But now it is here, if there were anything I could do to stop it, I would.

She will never return my Attachment. Not just because she is human or because she does not feel for me. She does. But because it is impossible for us. Even if our species can form an alliance, it does not mean lifelong union could ever be possible between two groups with our history.

My family, my warriors, would never accept her. I would have to betray them to be with her.

But I have no control over myself in this. I am powerless against fate and my instinct.

There is only one step left: a willingness to sacrifice my life for hers. Once I value her life more than my own, I will know I have lost my soul to her.

And there will be no way to get it back.

Once complete, the only way to end the Attachment is death.

I am stunned to feel tears dripping onto her cheeks.

"What's wrong?" I ask.

She looks at me with a sadness in her eyes. "I don't know."

Chapter Twenty-Five

Nemona

It's a lie.

I know why I'm crying, but I'm not brave enough to tell him.

I can barely tell myself.

I haven't had a family, or I should say, allowed myself to have a family since my parents died. I think my crew wanted to be my family; I see that now. But part of the reason I made everyone hide their identities was so I didn't get too close to them. I didn't want the risk of losing them.

If I kept them at a distance, I didn't have to expose myself to the possible pain that would come if they died or left or rejected me.

But to feel the strength of Oten's Attachment...

Whatever Koviye did to us, his light joined us somehow, letting us not just feel but experience each other's feelings. And Oten's feelings for me—I don't know how he's been hiding them.

They are consuming. The Attachment may not be something he'll ever let go of.

It saddens me. I mourn, for him.

Because this can never work.

We are too different. Not only two different species, but too different in what we want from the world. He wants to protect his people, to maintain his home. I want to explore the universe.

Not to mention him being near immortal and me being mortal. I will die and leave him.

Losing me is going to cause him the kind of pain that could ruin him.

It would break not just his heart but his very being.

I don't want him to hurt. I don't want to be the reason why he could be damaged beyond repair.

To reject him would be a crime.

What he feels for me is so pure, so void of selfish goals or plans. He told the truth when he said I didn't know what he wanted. Next to what he feels for me, he couldn't care less about ever having a family.

He cares about me.

He loves me.

With everything he has.

It's so strong. His need to protect me is a force of nature. I felt it in me like a blow. But he's kept it leashed out of respect for me.

If I needed him, all I would have to do is tell him, and he would give himself. Anything. Everything. His Attachment isn't complete yet, but it could be.

It awes me, and I bury my face in his chest, trying to contain my emotions. Feeling his love for me caresses a place inside me—the need to be loved—that I buried decades ago along with my parents.

I'll have to bury it again.

I collect myself, putting my emotions back where they belong, and ease myself out of his arms.

He brushes his knuckles over my cheek. "Are you sure you don't know what's wrong?" I can see it in his eyes, he's suspicious. He suspects I'm lying.

But I can't tell him. I can't hurt him. So rather than lie again, I just shake my head. "I can't."

I pull away from him so I can stand and put my uniform back on.

He helps me, as much as I let him.

Koviye, who's been politely giving us privacy, while still shedding his light on us, asks, "Are you okay?" He's somber, his joviality gone, as though he knows the intimacy he has caused—the intensity of the moment that he enhanced between us.

Neither Oten nor I answer. I don't know how to express how I feel.

"It happens sometimes," Koviye says gently. "The light creates a unity between lovers if there is an emotional affinity."

"Sometimes?" Oten asks with a note of bitterness. "You could have warned us."

"If I had realized there was such a connection between you, I would have. But to be clear, what you felt was true." He folds his arms. "I cannot create feelings. I only magnify what's already there."

I'm too emotionally raw to talk about it or be angry at Koviye for doing that to us. Oten seems to be, too, so we follow Koviye in silence.

The first rays of sunlight peek through the trees. We march on through the jungle in Koviye's path. It's no longer a bushwhacking situation. We've met up with a road of sorts. It carves through the trees and is packed tight with a light-colored surface material.

"A transport should pass by to give us a ride into the town soon," Koviye says, and he begins to hum.

The commlink on my wrist lights up multiple times. My crew has noticed I'm missing and is trying to contact me. I respond to let them know I'm all right and will return when I can. I don't give them details. I don't want to risk them coming after Oten.

Though they may suspect what I have done.

I'll contact them again once we find the Fellamana civilization.

Oten asks him questions about the Fellamana, and I'm surprised I didn't think to ask or take the opportunity to learn the customs and culture of his species. But I forgot. I'm too wrapped up in the feelings coursing through me.

A bitterness rises in me. An anger at Koviye for whatever he did that revealed Oten's feelings to me when I didn't need to know them.

"What did you do to us?" I bite out at Koviye. "That thing with your light when it—" I don't want to admit how much it made me feel.

"Let me think of a word that might translate." With the coming day, he no longer shines like a light, but his whole body is as translucent as an old-fashioned lightbulb. "We call it the unionizer? The union-maker? Something like that. It unites lovers so they can feel not only each other's pleasure but each other's feelings."

"All Fellamana can do this?" Oten asks.

Koviye preens. "Some. But not all." He glances at us. "I didn't realize what was happening until it was too late. I would've stopped if I'd known." He looks forward and keeps walking. "On the positive side, it should have satisfied your *desidre* even more so you can go without sex for longer, if you choose."

"Good," I breathe on instinct, grateful to get a break

from how much I need Oten. Except, it doesn't feel that way in my body. Maybe it'll change, like Koviye says.

But Oten's gaze falls to the ground, and he puts some distance between us. I've hurt him.

Did he like the connection Koviye made between us? But how could he? He must have felt how my feelings for him run nowhere near as deep as his for me.

"How fast can you get us to your communication center?" I ask Koviye. That's the reason I'm on this trip. I really should get back to my crew. I don't need to stay with Oten.

But my stomach twists to the point of making me sick.

Am I really planning to leave him with the Fellamana?

He'd certainly be safer than with my crew.

But I would never see him again. For certain.

My skin goes clammy, and a feeling of morbid regret creeps through my veins. I'll remember him the rest of my life.

I know that with certainty.

He's awakened me. To myself. To my body. To my desires and, in many ways, who I am.

How can I just plan to leave him?

But I'll have to. His crew will come to get him, and he'll leave. His promise to help with repairs of the *Origin* will never happen. His Attachment to me has him delusional about what is possible with the other Ssedez.

None of this can end happy. Except maybe Oten getting away from here alive.

A vehicle with other Fellamana stops to give us a ride. It glides along the smooth road surface almost in a hover, on something much more advanced than a wheel. The underside of it vibrates too fast for me to see anything but a black blur, but the sound it makes is like a calming low wind, not a noisy engine.

I would normally ask questions, but I'm floundering in

my own feelings of…grief, disappointment, confusion? I don't know what they are.

Oten asks questions for us, being as polite as I'm unable to be.

Koviye translates and introduces us to the other Fellamana in the vehicle, all as iridescent and glowing as he is. Though none of them seem to glow with precisely the same translucent rainbow. Different color palettes spread from their veins—some purples, some blues, some greens.

They greet us in a similar way he did Jenie, though likely on a less intense level—a friendly grip of the forearm and a burst of pleasurable light from their fingertips. It makes shaking hands seem like a gift of positive feelings.

We roll into their town, their streets lined with buildings as clear as they are. The walls are all made of a glass-like material. Everything within them is visible. Including—

I stare, disbelieving what I'm seeing, then pull my gaze away, not wanting to be rude.

Koviye gives me a mischievous grin. "Go ahead and watch. That's what they want."

I glance up and see it again in another building. "Do the Fellamana just…"

"When you live in a jungle that releases a toxin if you don't have sex, what kind of society were you expecting?"

Oten tilts his head while he stares. "It is erotic." He glances at another couple, visibly copulating behind a see-through wall.

Oh, wait. A third person raises their head. I guess not a couple, a ménage.

"We enjoy our voyeurism," Koviye says. "So look your fill. They wouldn't do it in full view if they didn't like being watched."

I see another scene: this one not just visible but literally up against a wall. An ass pressed against the glass, with not one, but two people on their knees in front of the person.

Koviye leans closer to us. "If you stay long enough, you'll get to see our Sex Games."

"Sex Games?" Oten asks, a smile lifting his cheeks.

"It's a tournament of sorts, lovers displaying their sexual prowess. Extra points for the more creative and kinky." Koviye wags his eyebrows at me.

And I have to laugh. "That sounds fun actually."

Oten leans into me and says, "It's just what you wanted, right? To learn about societies less rigid in their sexual norms than humans."

"It is." I glance at Koviye and decide I should give him the gratitude he deserves. "Thank you for bringing us here."

"The pleasure is mine, I assure you." He points to the Fellamana whom our transport is passing, all of them staring at us as we go. "You will be quite the exotic attraction. Everyone will be clambering for a chance to watch you feed the *desidre*. If you're up for an audience."

"Really?" I ask.

"It's not often we get to watch another species copulate. And two different species at once." He shivers with delight. "Leave your curtains open, and you'll be the star of the show."

The transport drops us at the town's communication center. Oten learns how to operate it and manages to connect with his ship.

They'll be here to get him tomorrow.

Tomorrow!

It slams me like a fist to the gut.

I'm losing him.

Chapter Twenty-Six

Oten

Gahnin, my second-in-command, answers with as much enthusiasm as I thought he would. He had assumed me dead, and he apologizes for not sending a search party to Fyrian for me.

There's nothing to forgive, given our assumptions that the planet's atmosphere would have killed anyone who entered it.

They will send a landing ship to the coordinates I give them for the Fellamana's landing pad tomorrow.

I do not mention Nemona or the humans. It'll be much easier to explain everything face-to-face.

I finish the communication and expect Nemona to be excited. Help for her ship is arriving tomorrow. Instead, her expression is like I just told her someone died.

"What's wrong?" I ask her.

She chews her jaw then says, "Tomorrow is very soon."

"The sooner they're here, the sooner we can see what supplies we have that can help repair the *Origin*."

"You're delusional." She walks away from me, before I can explain she is wrong. That I am the commander of the Ssedez warriors. My authority has been untested for a century.

They follow my orders without question. Their trust in me is absolute. And once they see the truth of the mistake we made in attacking the *Origin* and their true mission, they will be as driven to make amends as I am.

We share a meal with the Fellamana in a grand hall. The ceiling is a myriad of extravagant colors, and the walls are made of their kind of glass. It has cooling qualities each time I get near a wall, which, given they are surrounded by hot jungle, is good.

They flood us with questions about the Ten Systems. Nemona's melancholy seems to lift, or at least she hides it, and is generous with her inside information about the Ten Systems' military. Which is as invaluable to me as it is to the Fellamana.

That and I am riveted watching her talk tactics and hearing her divulge her impressive range of experience. What she had to go through to achieve the status of general in the Ten Systems' ranks, and so young—she is one of the bravest people I have ever encountered.

The twin suns descend over the horizon, and Koviye excuses us on account of our lack of sleep.

He leads us down a peaceful street, dim in the twilight, toward our private resting quarters. A few Fellamana mill around, and an occasional transport floats softly by. I have never seen a private vehicle move with such quiet. I will be studying their engines and how they are fueled before we leave here.

"This is it." Koviye stops in front of an empty glass building. The lights are on, but no one is inside.

A scream shatters the quiet, then a loud pop sounds, like

an explosion.

I look up and see one of the Fellamana transports smoking and out of control—speeding like a bullet—toward Nemona.

It is a surreal experience. But one that activates pure instinct.

No thought enters my head except *save her*.

It comes from a primal place inside me that is incapable of making judgment or decision. Only action.

"Run!" Koviye shouts.

But I go in the opposite direction. I jump in front of Nemona and take the full impact of the vehicle to the center of my back. It crushes instantly, as it would against a cement wall. Also by instinct, my natural armor sprouts in time so that the vehicle gives me no physical harm. But I do not expect the fire that erupts from the vehicle next. My armor is impervious to a lot of things, but fire is not one of them.

I leap back from the flames just before the vehicle implodes on itself.

It sits in a pile of black ash on the pavement.

That is a serious design flaw in whatever is powering those vehicles. Luckily it appears no one was inside.

"What was that?" Nemona shouts and shoves me from the side.

I stumble backward. "Excuse me?"

"Who the hell do you think you are? Jumping in front of me like some overgrown hero." Her eyes are alight with fury, and she shakes her head. "You're a goddamn fool."

I glance back at the pile of smoking black ash and realize, she is right.

"That thing could've burned you alive!" she cries with such force I cringe. "Why didn't you get out of the way like the rest of us?"

"Because…" It was heading straight toward her.

"Did you think I wouldn't move?" she says, baffled at my stupidity.

It is laughable.

Of course, she was going to get out of the way. Of course, there was no way it would have hit her. She is fast. She is strong. I know this. She needed no assistance from me.

Why did I do that?

I feel it then.

For the first time in my life.

It is like every puzzle piece inside me slipping into its rightful place. Every vacancy in me filling with a wholeness, and there is a burn in my chest. Not like the *desidre*, not the painful kind of burn.

This is a heat, the kind that creates life and stops time and can remake the world.

It floods me, and I feel a wash of strength I have never felt before. Like my whole body has solidified into a weapon.

"You're shining," Nemona mutters, and I find her staring at me.

I look down and the brightness of my armor is—glittering. Sparkling like it's been implanted with a thousand diamonds.

I have to close my eyes and clench my jaw to keep from screaming.

The Attachment. The final step—the willingness to sacrifice my life for hers.

It is complete.

I can feel it like an invisible cord that's implanted in my gut as though it runs from me and wraps around her. Except, even though I can't see it, I feel it as though it is as real as the stars in the sky: my connection to her.

It is irrevocable.

It is done.

She owns me now. Heart, soul, and body.

For the rest of my life, I will be unable to procreate with

any other. I will physiologically be incapable of taking any other lover.

And she does not want me.

She will never return the Attachment. My people will never accept her, a human, as my mate.

Koviye is talking, saying something about apologies and explanations for the vehicle malfunction. Other Fellamana come, emergency responders, to clean up the mess.

My brain is in a haze, and I am incapable of thinking anything other than—

I must have her.

If the *desidre* made my desire for her intolerably intense, this—the Attachment—is like my carnal self needs to be one with her. Not just physically. But in spirit, too.

The need for her to accept me feels like the only thing I have ever wanted or will ever want again. My ability to fight it or be in denial about it is at an end.

It is over. My life no longer belongs to me. It is hers.

And there is nothing I can do but pray she will not destroy me for it.

Eventually, Koviye leads us inside to our apartment. I follow him, numb, unable to speak much.

Inside, the center room that's most visible has a bed and various odd-shaped pieces of furniture—which I imagine work well for various sex positions.

"Anyone and everyone can see us here," Nemona says.

Koviye gestures toward the enclosed walls in the center. "There are inner rooms for privacy. Though it would win you better favor with the Fellamana if you respect the custom. It shows trust to allow others to watch you in your intimate moments.

"And it's part of how we judge character. How one makes love reveals a lot about who you are."

"Who says there'll be any lovemaking going on?" Nemona snaps, and I cringe.

Her denial, it physically hurts me now. Like a blow to the chest.

"I'll leave you to work that out." Koviye laughs and closes the door behind him.

Nemona and I are completely alone for the first time since the cave.

"So, what's with you?" she asks cautiously. But the way she keeps her distance from me, I think she knows.

I clear my throat, and I am unable to speak above a whisper, "It is finished. I—" I swallow and force the words out. "I am complete."

"What does that mean?" Her voice shakes with nerves.

I turn away from her and stare out the window. "Do not ask about things you do not want to hear." She loathes the mere mention of the Attachment.

She is silent long enough that I look over to be sure she is still there.

She is staring at me. And the sight of her—she is beauty and strength personified. I cannot feel remorse for my Attachment being for *her*. There is no one I have met who I hold with such value. I have only remorse for the hard truth that this can never be.

"I'm going to go sleep," she says and moves toward the inner rooms, hidden from the windows.

It's reasonable considering we got none last night.

"I'm tired, too." I follow her. Not following her for me, in the state I am in, is impossible.

She stops but doesn't look at me. "Alone."

It cinches my lungs. She's entitled to her space, but she says it with such severity, it sounds like more than temporary.

I do not know how I will survive it—being separated from her.

Normally, among the Ssedez, when the Attachment completes itself, the lovers are given quarantine and not disturbed or separated for days, weeks. They are allowed to satisfy the frenzy that begins without interruption.

But that only works when the other returns the Attachment.

Which she never will.

I stroke a hand over her back. "I'll be here when you want company."

She squares her shoulders and faces me. "We should end this now. It'll be easier than doing it tomorrow when your crew is here."

I force myself to breathe through the panic her words cause me. "You cannot mean that." Not after what happened in the jungle. Not after she showed me what she feels for me, after how much she knows I feel for her. She cannot possibly just…end this.

"It's pointless. You'll be going home with your warriors. I'll go back to the *Origin*."

I do not care about logistics. All I know is separation is not an option. "I am not leaving you."

Her look is all doubt. She doesn't believe a word I say. "You have to."

"Nemona." The pleasure I get in saying her name sends ripples down my spine. "You do not understand. I am incapable of leaving you."

"Bullshit!" she snaps.

My heart races. Her words inflict pain on me like knife wounds. "I assure you, it is not bullshit. It is very real."

"But I don't love you!" she all but screams.

It sends a shock of hope through me.

The intensity she says it with means her feelings for

me run deeper than she knows. "You can't hide from me, Nemona. I saw inside your heart. I know what's in here." I press my palm to the center of her chest.

She pushes my hand away. "It doesn't matter what's in there. I'm incapable of feeling those things. For anyone. I'm a military woman. That's what I do. Relationships don't work for me. I don't have a family. I don't have friends."

"*That* is bullshit. You love your crew. They are your family."

"No." She shakes her head; she will not look at me. "That's not how this works. We are military. We are—"

"You're not in the military anymore!"

"I am!" Fury—or panic—pours from her eyes. "I will never be anything else. Don't you understand? Pieces of me died with them. And those pieces are never coming back."

I squint at her, confused. "Them? As in your parents? You think your ability to form relationships died with them?"

"I know it did!"

How do I convince her her heart was never broken? Only wounded. She still thinks it's in pieces. "You were left alone. With no one."

"I'm still alone. And I will die alone. That's how this works."

"It does not have to be this way." I try to reach for her, but she pushes my hand out of the way.

"Stop it." She dances away from me and rubs the bridge of her nose. "These conversations are meaningless. In fifty years, I'll be too old to do battle while you'll still be waging war against the Ten Systems."

My heart stops. I had not allowed myself to think about it. To watch her grow old and die, then to go on living without her... It is like sliding a blade between my ribs and twisting it all around my heart.

My second-in-command, Gahnin, lost his mate in the

war against the Ten Systems. The torture he went through is not something I wish on anyone. Least of all myself.

Her eyes close, and she takes a deep breath. "You don't want to watch me die. So even if I could return your feelings, which I can't, this can never work." She reopens her eyes and looks away.

But I force myself to breathe and my heart to restart. "It can," I whisper, unable to process the possibility that we cannot work. We have to. It is not only the Attachment that makes me need her anymore. From the depths of my soul, I want to be with her.

"I can't grow old and fade and watch you never change."

I drop my gaze to the floor. She is right. I could never ask her to do that.

She steps closer, and her voice softens further. "Your people will never allow you to be with a human."

I have to say it. I cannot hold it in. "You do not have to be mortal if you do not want to be."

Her eyes widen, but I cannot watch the disgust that will come over her after that. I cannot begrudge her her desire to remain human, but it doesn't mean I have to witness her revulsion at becoming like me.

I retreat from her and go to one of the inner rooms—and close the door.

I am too much of a coward to watch her leave me. It would rip me in two.

Chapter Twenty-Seven

Nemona

He's right.

When I woke up Ssedez last week, it was a shock I wasn't expecting. But if someone asked me, would you like to live a thousand years, would I, could I, say *no*?

The chance to stay in my prime for generations. To be strong enough to resist every weapon.

Why would I turn that down?

So much time to live would seem infinite. I would never stop learning, discovering, exploring. There would be no limits to what I could do.

But it doesn't mean I could ever feel what he feels. Not only because I was not born a Ssedez, but because I don't do love.

Even if I'm honest and admit that what I feel for him is infinitely more than I have ever felt for anyone, it still can't be. I would eventually lose him. And I can't take it. I lost the last person I loved a long time ago, and I could never go through that again. Except, he can't die. Or he can, but he's about as unkillable of a being as I'll ever meet. If there's anyone I could risk it with, it's him.

And if I let him go…

I'll never see him again.

The realization strikes through me like a lightning bolt to my heart.

I can't let him go. He's as much a part of me as my lungs, or the air I breathe. I ache not being near him, and not just for sex, but for not talking to him, for not seeing his warrior's stare grow soft when he looks at me. My arms feel empty without him to hold.

I can't let him go.

And because of the Attachment, he would never leave me.

The certainty fills my chest with a warmth I can barely stand. I have to sit down and close my eyes.

No fear of loss.

He would love me forever.

I know this. He is a surer force in my life than anything I have ever known. And he's offering it to me. He's looked his whole existence—centuries—for me.

All I have to lose is my humanity. But how much more do I have to gain…

The fear recedes. It separates and parts like a cloud blinding my view. And I discover what it was covering. All the feelings that I was trying not to feel.

All the love.

For him.

It fills me.

I'm not just capable of it. I have it in abundance. Enough to rival even his Attachment.

I rush back to the inner rooms and throw open the closed door.

He bolts upright on the bed. "What's wrong?"

My feet freeze to the ground, and my mouth opens on no words, but my heart thunders like it's bursting to be heard.

"I love you," I blurt so hard and so fast my mouth goes dry.

His stare is as intense and impenetrable as ever, and I'm terrified for a heartbeat that I'm too late. But he takes a heavy breath and intones in a deep whisper, "I love you, too."

I leap on him and kiss him. Wrap my arms and legs around him as tight as I can. I want to take him inside me and hold him there and never let him go.

"You'll never leave me. You won't die on me. You'll never stop loving me," I say, needing confirmation of what I've realized.

He grasps my hand and holds it over his heart. "I swear it, by every god there is. I will love you and never leave you."

"My parents," I gasp, my eyes filling with tears. "They died. They left."

"I cannot, will not ever." His gaze is so forward, so intense on mine. "Feel me. Feel my heart. It beats for you now. It always has. Though I did not know it." Then his tongue slides over some strange words I don't know. Something in his language.

"What does that mean?" I ask.

"It is hard to explain. The closest word you have for it is *eternity*. But it means more: my love and life without end is yours."

I see them—lowering past his upper lip—his fangs. I touch them, run my finger down the tip. "Saying it makes you want to bite me, doesn't it?" I can't stop my hands from shaking, knowing the permanence of the decision I'm about to make.

He doesn't try to hide his fangs from me. "It makes me want to make you mine. Permanently. To make you safe and protect you in the best way I can. So yes, it makes me want to bite you and fill you with all the strength I have to give you.

"But only if you want it." He takes a deep, shuddering breath. "If you want to stay human, I will love you no less."

I touch his fangs again, running my fingers up and down them.

His jaw shakes, and his breathing gets ragged.

I lower my mouth to his and lick one of his fangs from tip to root, tasting the tangy venom. He makes a low groan, and his hands clench in my sides, squeezing me like he's desperate to pull me to him.

I swallow the drops of venom, and it makes me shudder with him. He scratches my lip with the tip of his fang, and I take it in my mouth and suck on it, circling the tip with my tongue.

He clasps his arms around my back, and I straddle closer to him. His cock protests, hard and digging into my belly.

"Do you ever run out of venom?" I ask, breathing rushed.

"I've been saving up my venom my whole life for you."

"Really?"

"The venom only comes and my fangs only lower when I feel the Attachment."

That's new information. "You've never bitten anyone except me?"

"Except in my dreams when I'd wake up with my fangs aching—no." His gaze slides to my neck, and he fingers my pulse above my uniform collar.

I lower the zipper of my jacket and fold it back, exposing my whole neck. "How many times can you bite me in one night?"

His eyes widen. "I do not think there's a limit."

I lace fingers into his hair and raise my neck to his mouth. "I dare you to find out."

He needs no further urging.

He strikes, his fangs sinking into my flesh, and the sting is exquisite. The venom even more so.

It floods into me and shoots pleasure through my body. I arch against him, holding his head to my skin. He sinks his fangs deeper, until his lips meet my skin and his bite turns into the most blissful kiss.

I grind against his cock, needing him in me, rubbing against him between our clothes, wishing to hell and back I'd thought to get us naked first.

As though he can read my thoughts, he pulls his fangs out of me. I cry with the loss.

"It's all right. I'll bite you again." He licks my wounds closed.

I undo his pants and free his cock. I can't not hold it in my hand and stroke it.

He strips me of my uniform and, in a rush of brute strength, wraps my legs around him and slams my back against a wall.

And thrusts inside me.

I moan and cling to him.

He sinks his fangs into me again and fucks me ruthlessly.

It's just like the jungle, just like the *desidre*, except this time, it's all us. Nothing is doing this to us. It's really how he feels. This is how much he needs me and how much he's been holding back.

Maybe it never was the *desidre*. Maybe it was always just us from the beginning. I can't imagine, no matter how fierce the toxin, sex ever feeling this good, me needing it with every fiber of myself the way I do with him.

I'm helpless not to come—too fast. I wanted it to last.

But I don't have to worry.

The venom—I forgot—makes it go on and on. Wave after wave of ecstasy passing through my body in an endless tide. I feel it wash through him, and he pours all of his pleasure into me.

He's not done though. It's as though he'll never be done with me.

And I don't want him to be.

He fucks me again and again, every way a person can be fucked. We make it to the big room and give the Fellamana their show.

We sleep then do it again.

I lose track of how many times he bites me.

We turn on the lights so we can see each other—in truth, so we can watch me change.

It starts with the texture of my skin, then my gums begin to ache. He traces the little points; the fangs starting to poke through my upper jaw. They hurt, and he soothes them with his tongue. Whatever the healing properties it possesses makes the transformation easier.

By morning, I'm shining in glorious gold armor from crown to toe. I stand in front of the mirror admiring myself.

Oten looks, too, over my shoulder, and I watch his fangs descend, again.

"More?" I tease him.

He smooths his thumb beneath my upper lip to where my new fangs are starting to protrude. "More."

He strikes my neck, and I watch him in the mirror, sucking on me.

A thought occurs to me. If I'm getting fangs, I wonder if I could bite him, too. And with the thought, the strangest sensation starts in my mouth.

I moan and pull back my lip. It doesn't hurt. It's a relief, as though what really needed to happen was for me to let go.

My new fangs glide out of my gums, the points reaching my lower lip. They're not as long as Oten's.

"They'll get bigger," he says, breathless, watching me admire them in the mirror.

I touch them, stroke them with my tongue. "The venom!

I taste it!"

He growls a low throaty sound deep in his chest. "Yes. I hoped you would."

"You want me to bite you?"

He shudders, and his voice is tight with wanting. "Yes*sss*." His tongue lingers over the S in a needy hiss.

I turn to him, fingering his gold neck. "But can I? Will they be able to penetrate?"

"It's the only thing that can," he says. "Do you feel it?"

"Feel what?"

He lifts his brows like he's waiting for me to tell him.

I notice a vibration in my limbs, an intensity within my chest, a demand within my body that's new. It's an insatiable thing. Like being hungry, except in more than just my stomach. Like craving sex, but in more than just desire. It's…a completion. Of me.

Like my desire for him fills every vacant place in my heart and soul.

"The Attachment…" I whisper.

It has to be. When I look at him, the need in me starts to scream, my very skin pulsing like it will explode if I don't touch him and take him within me and keep him forever.

I could do battle. I could fight off a world of enemies to keep him safe.

The joy on his face is all-encompassing. He's wanted this, waited his whole life for this. Not just to feel the Attachment, but for someone to return it—and feel it for him.

The muscles in my limbs bunch and contract with a new kind of strength. It's inhuman, it's superior, it's…

Ssedez.

I grab him and slam him up against a wall. Able to move him with my new strength the way I never could before.

And sink my fangs into his neck.

Chapter Twenty-Eight

Oten

Her bite floods my veins with bliss, and I start to come without her even touching my cock. This, her wanting me this way, in this whole body, soul-consuming way—this is what I have craved for an eternity.

She bites me again and again. Relishing in her new fangs, in her new strength.

She dominates me—moving me how she wants me, and fucking me how she likes, and it fulfills a desire in me. One I knew I had but didn't know how to fulfill. Until her.

After who knows how many times, she slams my palms against the window, forcing me to look out at the crowd that has gathered, on the street, watching us.

She kneels in front of me, her back against the glass. She strokes my cock with her hand and sinks her fangs into my thigh.

I come, the way she knows how to make me. The silver liquid streams from my cock and splashes against the glass of the window. It sparkles and glows iridescent in the dark.

The crowd outside gasps and cheers so loud we can hear it through the window.

She laughs so hard, her fangs retract back into her gums. She stands, and I hold her against my chest, laughing with her.

"The Fellamana sure are easy to please," she chuckles.

"I think you might need to take a bow or something."

She turns and the crowd roars louder.

"Well done!" Koviye shouts from the door, entering.

"Is knocking not a custom among the Fellamana?" I say, trying to contain my annoyance of being disturbed.

"Why would I? You've already shown us everything. And what a show it was." He applauds, too. "I'd let you oblige them with an encore, but your Ssedez have landed, and I suspect you want to see them."

My chest grows tight. In all the pleasure of Nemona accepting me, loving me, and feeling the Attachment, I almost forgot about my warriors.

I do not know what they will think when they see her, or if they will accept my mate or not.

Nemona looks at me, her gold, sun-touched skin, the tone of a newly born Ssedez. I do not want to worry her with my fear. It will make no difference. If they do not accept her, then she and I will go elsewhere.

But that would mean leaving my warriors, my people.

My stomach twists, and I feel nauseous. I cannot imagine losing them.

A different kind of frustration is very clear in her expression. "I'm not sure if I'm capable of putting clothes on." Her new armor is too sensitive to touch anything.

"Who says you need to?" Koviye says. "I'll find you the lightweight Fellamana garments in the closet."

Nemona and I try on the traditional robes Koviye brings

us. They are so featherlight and flowing, it is as though we wear nothing. They are also entirely translucent.

"Why bother wearing them at all?" I ask.

"Beauty. Seduction." Koviye smiles.

I frown. "My warriors will be immensely confused."

Nemona's eyes widen. "I can't meet your soldiers like this. I have to wear my uniform."

"You could. It does betray you as a Ten Systems' soldier on sight, though."

She swears. "Then what the hell am I supposed to wear?"

I spy my leather pants lying on the floor of the bedroom. "You could go dressed as a Ssedez." She's worn them before. I remember her topless in the jungle, and I am hard again.

A smile creeps over her mouth as she nods. "Yes. That's the answer." She dons her utilitarian sports bra from her uniform and my leather pants, turned up on the ankles.

It does not matter what she is wearing. I will want to fuck her. But seeing her in that makes me *really* want to fuck her.

"And you?" Koviye smirks at me.

I scowl at him. I'd forgotten we weren't alone.

The humor in his expression makes me skeptical. Maybe this whole joke is on me. I push past him to inspect the closet myself. In the back, there's an opaque robe in a somber gray.

I pull it out and declare, "I'll wear this."

Koviye grimaces. "Do not wear that. Under any circumstances. Unless you are interested in having sex with no one."

Nemona laughs. "Well, I know that's not true, and I'm the only one who matters. So it's perfect."

Koviye groans loudly but concedes. "If that is your choice, follow me."

We travel to the landing pad on the edge of the jungle, passing several large Fellamana spacecraft. Their clear outer protective coating makes me wonder if the Fellamana ability to disappear applies to their technology as well.

The sight of the Ssedez ship—a stealthy, shining obsidian—is like seeing a slice of home.

We get closer and beside the open door stands my second-in-command, in many ways my brother, and definitely best friend, Gahnin.

"Have they been given the *topuy*?" Nemona asks Koviye.

"The first thing we gave the whole crew on greeting," he says.

"Good," I say, grateful, and I leap from the Fellamana transport to greet my brother-in-arms.

Gahnin hugs me in a tight embrace. "Praise gods, you are alive," he greets me in Ssedez.

"And you." I lean back and hold his head in my hands. He holds mine, and we touch foreheads—in the way of our greeting.

"Did we lose any warriors?" I ask before I stand away from him.

He holds my shoulders and shakes his head. "No one. Our forces are undiminished. Our battle was successful." He gives a triumphant smile. "I saw the wreckage of the human ship on our way in. A pleasant sight to behold."

I stand back from him and give a saddened shake of my head. "It is not a pleasant sight. It is a tragedy. We were wrong."

"What?"

"We never should have attacked them. Not we. *I*." I lift my chin. "Never should have ordered the attack. They are a peaceful mission of explorers who rebelled against the Ten Systems' fleet. They are our allies, not our enemies."

The confusion on his face borders on anger. "They are humans. They are all the same. They are in a Ten Systems' ship. Who is *this*?" He spots Nemona, and his eyes light like stars.

I place a hand at the small of her back and switch to the human language so she will understand. "This is their general. The nexus of their rebellion."

"But..." Gahnin stutters with confusion, struggling to switch languages. "She—is Ssedez. There were Ssedez among the crew?"

She speaks, and her human accent makes it clearer than I could. "I am Nemona, general of the Ten Systems' starship *Origin*. We rebelled and escaped the fleet two months ago. To our knowledge, they have no idea of our whereabouts. Our mission is one of peaceful exploration, and we would be honored to make an alliance with the Ssedez."

"An alliance?" Gahnin almost laughs. "We destroyed your ship. Your species annihilated a million Ssedez. And how..." He looks at me with disbelief. "Why does she appear Ssedez?"

I put my arm around her, and in the way of our people, I let my fangs descend, still begging to be unleashed even after biting her an uncountable number of times.

He gasps. He knows what it means, emotionally.

My palm sweats in contact with Nemona's shoulder. No amount of military orders from me can force Gahnin to accept my human mate. The loss of his own mate will not make this easy.

He stares at her, his expression going icy cold and unreadable. He turns his face away, staring off toward the jungle, as though he cannot bare to look at her.

My heart sinks, and cracks a little. He's not going to accept her. He's—

"Felicitations, Commander," he says in the human language so Nemona can understand. He turns back to me and bows his head in respect. "It is a special day."

His expression is anything but joyous. But I see it for what it is now.

Pain. It hurts him. To see me with a mate brings up his own mourning.

His gaze is all he wishes to say to me in private. He knows, better than anyone, how I have searched and the importance of what the Attachment means.

"Nemona is—was—human," I say. "But my venom has changed her. She is both human and Ssedez now."

He puts a fist to his chest. "It is so." His gesture is an age-old sign of trust among us. He glances back at the other warriors being greeted by the Fellamana. "It may take more time to convince them. But we will."

"They will understand. They must." I relax my possessive hold on Nemona. "I have promised—in order to atone for our mistake—we will help repair the *Origin*."

"She needs a new reactor," Nemona says.

Gahnin addresses Nemona. "I would make good on this promise. But our ship sustained damage to our reactor as well during the battle. We are not equipped to help with your repairs."

"Then we will travel home to retrieve what we need," I say. "Nemona, will you come with me?"

There's an excitement in her face at the mention. "To your world?"

"Yes. Meet the Ssedez. We will gather what we need and come back here."

"I'll have to communicate with my crew and let them know where I'm going."

"They will be okay without you for a time." I clasp our hands together. "I want you to see my world. Our world."

"And meet new friends," she says with a smile.

I hold her to me. "Your new family."

Epilogue

Nemona

Oten and I spend the day acquainting his warriors with the Fellamana. They're as shocked as they are intrigued by their lifestyle. Some of them even appear eager to...well, get down and dirty at the invitations from our new alien friends. It makes me wonder if all the Ssedez are as traditional and prone to monogamy as Oten, or if that's just him.

The warriors are wary of me but cordial. Oten assures me they would never go against him and openly reject me, but it will take time before they accept me. Which is fine. My crew treated Oten far worse.

I communicate with Jenie via the commlink on my wrist. She's mad as hell at me for disappearing. But I don't feel guilty until she says, "I've been worried sick. The Ssedez escaped. Did he come after you?"

I didn't tell her he was with me. Damn. "I am safe. With him, Jenie. He's my friend."

Oten grunts beside me and gives me this look like, *Is that a joke?*

I take a deep breath. "Jenie, there's a lot I haven't told you." *Like the fact I'm not human anymore.* "And I need you to listen with an open mind."

"A Ssedez ship landed this morning," she says with some panic. "Did you see it? Are they after you?"

"No, they're…" I decide the best way to communicate how deeply I'm in this is to turn on the vid lens and show her what I look like. I select the button, and Jenie's image pops up in the miniature screen on my wrist.

I get to witness her shocked expression and gasp at my new appearance. I hadn't expected to feel hurt, but I do. I've made this change with pride, and I want it to be a happy thing where people congratulate me. I need to accept that joy isn't going to be anyone's first reaction.

Beside me, Oten clasps my free hand. He knows. He shares my joy. That's what matters.

"Nemona," Jenie breathes in a frightened whisper. "What did they do to you?"

I tell her the whole story: Oten's misunderstanding in thinking we were Ten Systems, how he accidentally turned me Ssedez the first time, how remorseful Oten is now that he knows our true mission. Then I drop the bomb that despite everything, I am in love with him and I chose to let him change me.

It's a relief to tell someone, and even though Jenie is skeptical, she listens without interrupting.

"You have some time to digest all of this," I conclude. "I'm going with Oten to his world to retrieve all the supplies we'll need to repair the *Origin*."

"He's going to help us?"

"To make amends for his mistake in attacking us, yes. We are going to be allies." I say it with the stern authority. There will be no argument on this when I get back.

I expect some pushback, a defensive response.

She's quiet for a moment, examining me, mulling my words. "Do you want backup?"

"For what?"

"To accompany you. Shall I send some of our crew with you? No matter how much you trust him, I'd rather you weren't alone." She wouldn't say that unless she believed me. She trusts me. She's not clouded with judgment over my choices.

I should've known she'd react so well. This is Jenie after all, and I'm a little ashamed at my lack of faith in her. "Thank you. I appreciate that, but we need to leave tonight. I'll return as soon as I can. We need the *Origin* back in the air."

"Yes, we do." She scrubs a hand over her face. "This is all great news, I suppose. It's just going to take some time to sink in. So you're staying with the—Felanema?"

"The Fellamana. Yes. They're a generous peace-loving people."

"Have you—I mean—there was one of them who was here. I think." She bites her lip as though holding back something.

I crack a half smile, unsure if I should let her know I witnessed her "greeting" with Koviye that night. "Koviye is here. I'm sure he'll come back. He's our translator after all. You'll see him again."

"Oh." She clears her throat and says too quickly, "It makes no difference to me if he comes back. I just wanted to know if you'd met him."

She wishes me luck on my journey, and I promise to contact her as soon as I return.

My final communications complete, Oten makes the decision that Gahnin along with a group of warriors will remain with the Fellamana to become acquainted and build alliances between their species.

I'm sure the warriors will enjoy the delights of the Fellamana immensely.

Except for one. I'm surprised that Gahnin wants to stay since he's as stalwart and uninterested in their charms as Oten. But it's agreed on, and, before dark, we take off for Oten's home without Gahnin.

I ask Oten why he left him behind when they seem so close.

"For one, he is my second-in-command," Oten says but looks away without finishing.

"And the other reason?"

He places a hand on my shoulder. "Gahnin's mate died. He's been alone for a century. Seeing me with you is difficult for him in ways that have nothing to do with which species you are. There's also the fact that his mate was killed by humans during the war."

I rub my face. "I can definitely see why he wouldn't want to be around me just now."

We strap into comfortable seats for takeoff. The ship is vastly different from the Ten Systems' ships, the only ones I've ever known. Those were utilitarian, metal, gray, no decorations, serving only efficient military purpose.

The Ssedez ship is designed with care and detail, decorated with paints and patterns, adorned with art and furniture, all reflective of a rich culture. I'd be in awe if I wasn't so anxious.

I'm filled with a dread though, as we're leaving the atmosphere—what if all this unfailing desire I'm feeling for Oten is just because of Fyrian? Off the planet, my military bioengineering could reassert itself, stealing my sexual desire with it—the way I've lived for a decade and a half.

Oten reaches for my hand. The ship groans from takeoff, too loudly for me to hear his voice as it breaks through the planet's atmosphere, but he gives me a calming look. Almost like he can read my fear about whether or not we'll feel the same when freed of the desire toxins.

There's a fierceness to his gaze, a certainty. His feelings will remain unchanged, and I believe him. I trust him. It's my body I don't trust.

The ship's acceleration reaches a peak then skyrockets into the weightlessness of space—and goes silent.

I love that, the experience of leaving a planet and entering the infinite. But I don't get time to enjoy it.

An alert sounds beside Oten, and he presses a button. An image of Gahnin pops onto the console screen, and Oten greets him in Ssedez.

Gahnin's expression is tight with anxiety. "General Nemona, another human has wandered in from the jungle. She is far gone with the fever of the *desidre*, and the Fellamana are taking her to receive medical care."

I sit up closer to the screen. "Is she there? Can I see her?"

He turns his device to the side and an image of an unconscious human woman, sweat running down her face, her complexion pinkened as though overheated. I recognize her and relief fills my chest.

"Assura!" I brush my fingers over the screen wishing I could touch her. "Oh, thank gods. Gahnin, will she live?"

He turns the camera back on himself. "I believe so."

Oten speaks up. "Gahnin, stay with her. You hear me? You will watch over her care personally. When she is healed, you will accompany her return to the humans."

A grimace flashes over Gahnin's face, but he recovers his composure. "Understood."

They hang up, and I glance at the commlink still on my wrist. "I should've left this so they could communicate with my crew. I can't even tell Jenie that Assura is alive, because it's out of range off-planet."

"Do you want to turn back?"

"No. Koviye will show Gahnin where to take Assura."

Oten rests his hand on my leg. "She'll be all right."

But I'm not listening to his words. I stare at his hand, the heat of his palm radiating onto my leather-clad thigh and traveling to my center. It storms through my core and reawakens my desire as though I haven't had sex with him in weeks. Or ever.

I feel my fangs lowering. They prick my lip, and I glance at his throat. I want to pierce him, to devour him. And then I want him to fuck me until there is nothing separating us. No fears about his people or mine, of whether they will accept us, of whether we are making the right decisions to lead them. All of that gone, lost in the thrill of his body taking over mine.

Him in me and I in him.

I guess my worry about my bioengineering interfering with my sex drive was baseless.

"See," his tone comes in a guttural rasp. "Nothing to worry about." He slips his fingers in my hair and urges my mouth toward his throat.

Not only does this desire never wane, it's endless. It'll take more than a lifetime to slake it. Good thing I'm Ssedez now, and I've got ten lifetimes.

It still won't be enough.

Acknowledgments

Thanks to Alexis Daria, for getting me into reading about sexy aliens—and for too many other priceless things to count.

Thanks to my agent, Rachel Brooks, for her unceasing support and faith in my work.

Thanks to Tracy Montoya, my editor, for making sure Oten and Nemona had to work for their HEA and that it wasn't just all sexy times.

Thanks to my PWG buds, Jenny and Nina, for early reading and laughs and company every week. To #RWchat and especially, C. L. Polk and Kimberly Bell.

To my husband, for recognizing that writing romance is almost as priceless to me as he is.

And to Bronwen Fleetwood, for reading anything and everything I have to throw your way—and for supporting it with such patience and care.

Reader, thank you for reading, for loving romance, and for going on the off-planet journey with me. I'd love to share more stories with you. I'm writing little tidbits and sending them to my mailing list all the time. Come along for the ride, if you haven't already, http://robinlovett.com/contact/.

Until next time…happy reading!

About the Author

Robin Lovett enjoys trips to alien worlds to avoid earthly things, like day jobs and housework. When not reading romance with her cat, she's busy writing sexy books, which may or may not involve anti-heroes, aliens, or both, but almost always enemies-to-lovers. She's a big fan of her husband who regards writing romance as far more important than practical things, like paychecks. Her favorite surprise in the world, or the universe, was finding out by some miracle other people want to read the same kind stories she loves to write. You can reach her on Twitter @LovettRomance or on Facebook @LovettRomance to chat or share ideas about what to put in the next story.

Stay tuned for more **Planet of Desire** *stories!*

CAPTIVE DESIRE
Coming in 2018!

and

DREAMING DESIRE

If you love erotica, one-click these hot Scorched releases...

Brazilian Fantasy
a *Dossier* novella by Cathryn Fox

When Piper finds herself in Brazil and sets eyes on the sexy billionaire her friends have in mind for her–she's all in. But there's a surprise she didn't count on. The dark and mysterious widower is so much more than she could ever imagined, and the chemistry between them is off-the-charts. And now he's using their two weeks to try to convince her to stay.

Five Ways 'til Sunday
a *Delta Blue* novel by Delilah Devlin

Jackson wants to marry Marti, but she's got a bucket list to complete before she ties the knot. A list of explicit sexual wishes no one man can fulfill. When Jackson finds out about Marti's list, he calls on his brothers in blue, four men he trusts with his life. He's sure the five of them can check off every item on Marti's list. But Marti has to agree to follow through—and he has to figure out if he can bear to share her.

Hold Me Harder
a *to Have and to Hold* novella by Renee Dominick

PR exec Natalie Lindgren thought she was past her days as a submissive. But that was before she ended up at one former Dom's ranch for her sister's pre-wedding getaway—and discovered the best man was a former Dom, too. How was she going to get through the weekend? Especially when it seemed unlikely that she'd end up on top…

Rescued by the Space Pirate
Part One of *Ruby Robbins' Sexy Space Odyssey* by Nina Croft

Ruby Robbins has always dreamed of going to space. So when she's approached to help her country—by going undercover in an alien slaver ship—she jumps at the chance. She never expects her biggest challenge will be fighting off a sexy space pirate determined to save her. Or that she'll enjoy the struggle quite so much…

Printed in Great Britain
by Amazon